As he swung her around, she caught a quick glimpse of Nicole, and then suddenly Mark pulled her toward him and kissed her. Not a stage kiss. Not a light brush of the lips. But a genuine, honest boy/girl kiss.

Mollie was stunned. It had happened so quickly she couldn't have done anything to prevent it even if she'd wanted to. And as it left her with a wonderful, tingling sensation, she wasn't sure she *would* have wanted to.

At that moment the song ended, and Mollie came to her senses and bolted up to her bedroom. She couldn't stay at the party one second longer. The kiss that she'd dreaded for so long had finally happened, and it changed everything. It felt natural, as if she'd known exactly how to do it all this time.

Most important, it felt good, and Mollie was very very scared of what might happen if Mark kissed her again.

FAWCETT GIRLS ONLY BOOKS

Sisters

THREE'S A CROWD #1

TOO LATE FOR LOVE #2

THE KISS #3

SISTERS

THE KISS

Jennifer Cole

FAWCETT GIRLS ONLY • NEW YORK

RLI:
VL: Grades 5 + up
IL Grades 6 + up

Library of Congress Catalog Card Number: 86-80878

ISBN 0-449-13008-8

Manufactured in the United States of America

First Edition: June 1986

Chapter 1

The pounding was the first thing Mollie Lewis heard when she woke up that Monday morning. Thump thump, thump thump. It sounded like a giant sledgehammer, but it was actually her heart—beating hard enough to wake her from a sound sleep. At first she thought it had something to do with the dream she'd just had. Then she remembered. Today was T-Day—Theater Day—the day she'd find out if she'd won a part in Vista High's fall musical production.

Ordinarily Mollie stayed in bed till the last-possible minute. But this morning she jumped up, washed her face, ran a comb through her long blond curls, and put on the first thing she grabbed from the closet. Then, still operating on fast forward, she raced downstairs to the kitchen.

Her fifteen-year-old sister, Cindy, looked up in

surprise. "Who wound you up this morning?" she asked, slipping off the earphones of her Sony Walkman.

Mollie ignored the question. Grabbing a bowl and spoon from the cabinet, she joined Cindy and their older sister, Nicole, at the large oak table that dominated the spacious room. "I'm so nervous I could eat every box of cereal in Santa Barbara!" she exclaimed.

"What gives?" Cindy asked. "Never mind, you don't have to tell me. It's a boy, right? Let me guess ... the cute blond who sat in front of us at the football game?"

"No, silly," Mollie retorted. "It's something even more important than boys. Today's *the* day. Tell her, Nicole." She looked expectantly at her seventeen-year-old sister, who was quietly scanning Barron's *Guide to Colleges*.

Nicole looked up from the book. "I don't know what you're talking about," she said. *"Je ne comprends pas."*

Mollie stared at her as if she'd just landed from Venus—and not because she'd spoken French. Nicole did that all the time. "What do you mean, you don't know? Have you forgotten about the auditions? Ms. Black is announcing who got the parts today!" She poured cereal into her bowl, nearly overflowing it.

"Actually, I *did* forget," Nicole said. She tossed back her straight brown hair with a flick of her hand. "But why are you nervous? I'll bet my French book you got the part."

"I only hope Ms. Black feels the same way," Mollie said as she poured milk into the bowl. This year's production was the musical comedy *Grease*, and she had tried out for the lead—Sandy—hoping that her enthusiasm would make up for her average singing voice. Absentmindedly she dug her spoon into the bowl and shoved it into her mouth. The taste nearly made her gag. "*Yccch,* what is this stuff?" she asked.

"Lucky Charms," Cindy answered with a grin.

Mollie looked in horror at the box, then at her sister. "How can you eat this? It's got *sugar* in it and probably a zillion calories!"

Playfully, Cindy flexed her right arm. "A surfer needs her carbohydrates."

"Well, I don't." Mollie rose from the table, nearly tripping over the family dog, Winston. She fed her cereal to the garbage disposal, then took a carrot out of the refrigerator. "I can't afford to gain weight. The play notes Sandy is sweet, wholesome, and cute—not pudgy. If I get the part I'll have to go on a diet."

Her sisters laughed. "If I had a dime for every time you've said that. . . ." Cindy shook her head and her short blond hair danced. "Honestly, Mollie. I don't know why you bother."

Mollie *was* definitely more developed than the average fourteen year old, a fact emphasized by her petite five-foot frame. And the curve gave her the mistaken idea she was fat, especially when she compared herself with her sisters. Cindy, the tallest of the three, had a lean, athletic build, with

Nicole, with her dark hair and blue-gray eyes, had a classic beauty and stayed thin no matter what she ate.

Nicole folded her arms and looked at Mollie. "If I were you, *cherie*, I'd pay less attention to these mystic diets and more attenton to my clothes. For example, that dress looks awfully familiar. Didn't you wear it Friday?"

Mollie looked down. "Oh, no. I can't go to school like this! Everyone will notice and I'll just *die!*" She flung herself into a chair.

Cindy stared at her. "I can't believe you're making such a big deal over clothes!"

"Come on, Cindy. You know how much Mollie loves to act," Nicole said. "If you think this is something, you should have seen her when she auditioned! I could tell Ms. Black was really impressed, and unless there's a rule against giving the lead to a freshman, I'm sure Mollie got it."

"You gave a pretty good reading too, Nicole," Mollie said, forgetting her act.

Nicole shook her head. "In your eyes, maybe. But you know I just went to that audition to hold your hand. I wouldn't have tried out if Ms. Black hadn't dragged me onto the stage. And even if I get a part, I probably won't take it. Acting's just not in my blood."

"Don't be so modest; you'd be a natural," Mollie insisted. "Especially if Mark gets the male lead. I can see it now, girlfriend and boyfriend up on stage together." A horrified look crossed her face as she realized what she'd said. "Oh, no! Ms.

Black knows you two are a couple. She'll think it's adorable to pair you off on stage, too. I'm doomed!"

Cindy snorted. "Don't be so sure. I've heard Nicole sing." Then, as her older sister shot her a sidelong glance, she added quickly, "Of course, I'm no better. I always thought a tuning fork was something you ate with."

"Morning." Laura Lewis, the girls' mother, entered the kitchen and went straight to the coffee maker. "Did any of you girls feed the cats?

"I will." Cindy got up from the table. "We were just talking about what Mollie should wear when she gets her star on the Hollywood Walk of Fame."

Her mother looked blank.

"Today's the day Mollie begins her Vista High acting career," Nicole explained.

"Nicole, too," Mollie piped up.

"Forget it, Mollie. I intend to be in the audience watching you," Nicole said. She eased her chair back from the table. "I've got to be going. I have to check out some photos in the yearbook office before first period. See you later."

Mollie got up, too. "You guys had better go on without me," she said as she headed for the stairs. "I've got to change."

Unlike Cindy, Mollie was no athlete. But she felt she must have set a new speed record, dashing from the bicycle racks outside the stately, Spanish-style school building through the crowded halls to the auditorium. Unfortunately all she got for her effort was a sweaty brow and strange looks from the other students. There was nothing on the bulletin board next to the double-doored entryway except a hand-lettered sign that said "Beat West Side"—a reference to that weekend's football game against Vista's major rival.

Mollie wondered wildly if she had it all wrong and today wasn't the day the cast list would be posted. But just as she began to question her sanity, a few other students showed up—also looking for the list.

One of them was a somewhat overweight junior who introduced herself as Heather Wynn-Sommers. "I'm not surprised," she said with a deep sigh. "They don't call her the late Ms. Black for nothing."

Mollie was about to ask Heather what part she'd auditioned for, but just then the first bell rang and the girl strode away, and Mollie realized she'd better hurry off, too, if she didn't want to be late.

Twice during the morning Mollie dashed back to the auditorium between classes. But there was still no list posted. The tension of not knowing was beginning to make her head ache, and even though she tried to keep her mind on school and off theater, it was as difficult as keeping Winston's mind off food. Luckily, no one seemed to notice—until French I.

As her teacher Mrs. Preston started going over every possible conjugation of the verb *avoir*, Mollie fogged out, letting her mind replay her audition the week before, when she and Sam Yamaguchi had read a first-act scene from *Grease* together.

She'd known little about the play other than that it was a musical about the 1950s, but she wanted the lead more than anything. She knew she'd need an edge to win out over the upperclassmen who'd also be going after the role. So the night before the audition she'd gone up to the attic and dug out a box that contained her mother's high school memorabilia. She'd pored over the school newspapers and yearbooks to get a sense of what people looked like, and how they talked back then. She'd absorbed enough to make her feel she wouldn't embarrass herself on stage. But the question still remained: Had the extra effort paid off?

Right in the middle of her daydream, Mrs. Preston rapped her pointer against the chalkboard. "Mademoiselle Lewis," she called. "*Ou est* Mademoiselle Lewis?"

The titters from her classmates woke Mollie up. She took one look at her glaring teacher and blushed. "Yes, Mrs. Preston?"

"Mademoiselle Lewis, you and I have a contract. You've agreed to come to this room at this time every day, and I've agreed to make you understand French. I can't keep up my end of the bargain if you don't keep up yours. *Comprenez-vous?*"

"*Oui,* Madame Preston."

"Just to make sure, we'll talk about it after school," Mrs. Preston said firmly.

The bell cut off further discussion, and Mollie pounded a fist on her desk in frustration. In her short time at Vista, she had learned not to challenge her strict French teacher. Like it or not, she'd have to face her punishment, and she could only hope it wouldn't include a long lecture. Her idea of high school fun did not extend to lengthy student-teacher meetings.

Dejectedly, she walked into the hallway, followed closely by her friends Sarah and Linda.

"Tough luck in there," Linda said.

"Yeah, it easily could have been me," Sarah added. "I was daydreaming about Andrew. I'm seeing him next period."

"Say no more," Linda said. Andrew Wedekind was Sarah's latest crush.

Mollie mumbled a few words of encouragement, but her heart wasn't in it. She was too upset at herself for getting into trouble with Mrs. Preston. On top of everything else, Mrs. Preston was Nicole's favorite teacher, and if her sister found out, Mollie knew she'd be in for a double dose of reprimands for her inattention.

Her run-in with the teacher was still gnawing at her an hour later as she walked into the cafeteria for lunch. Grabbing a tray, she got in line, oblivious to the activity and chatter around her. Reminding herself she was on a diet, she reached for a garden salad and apple juice, paying the cashier with a five-dollar bill her mother had given her that morning. The cashier had to remind her to take the change. Finally she snapped out of the doldrums when she saw Sarah waving frantically at her from the back of the large, rectangular room. The tall brunette was smiling broadly, and Mollie figured that meant Andrew had asked her out—or, at the very least, talked to her.

Mollie set her tray on the formica tabletop across from her friend. "So when's the big date?" she asked.

Sarah's face fell. "What date?" she grumbled, casting a wary look toward the middle of the room where Andrew was seated.

"You mean he didn't ask you?"

Sarah shook her head glumly.

"There I go, sticking my foot in my mouth again," Mollie said with a sigh. "So why the sugar-coated grin?"

Sarah brightened. "It was for you, Mollie. Congratulations."

Linda, sitting alongside Sarah, leaned over and patted Mollie's arm. "Yeah, way to go," she said. "I knew you had it in you."

Mollie's eyes darted from one friend to the other. "What are you—" Then it dawned on her. "The cast list! It's up, isn't it?"

Sarah nodded, her blue eyes widening in surprise. "You mean you didn't know?"

"It wasn't there this morning," Mollie said.

"Well, I saw Ms. Black posting it on my way over here," said Linda. "Your name is next to Sandy. That's the part you wanted, isn't it?"

Mollie was so excited she clenched her jaws tightly together, afraid that if she opened her mouth she'd shout so loudly the whole school would hear her. "Sandy! I can't believe it," she finally managed to say. "I've got to see this for myself!" And, leaving her friends and her uneaten salad behind, she dashed off to the auditorium.

Linda was right. The cast list was there, and the first name at the top was Mollie Lewis, with "Sandy" typed a few spaces away. Mollie moved her index finger across the line, making sure that her eyes weren't playing tricks on her. But it was true. She was Sandy—or at least she would be when the play opened its three-night run.

Mollie sank down by the auditorium doors. She was too excited to go back to the cafeteria and needed time to compose herself. In her heart she'd known that, eventually, she'd land a role in a Vista High production. But she'd never figured it would happen so soon—in her freshman year. Realizing she'd beaten out dozens of upperclassmen made her proud—but nervous, too. Would she really be able to pull it off?

When she felt more in control of herself, Mollie got up and scanned the rest of the cast list. Most of the names meant nothing to her, since this was the first theatrical presentation of the year. But she recognized two: Heather, the girl she'd met that morning, had landed the role of Sandy's friend Jan. And Nicole's boyfriend, Mark, would be playing Danny, the male lead. Unfortunately, Nicole's name was nowhere on the list.

I hope she doesn't mind, Mollie thought. But she knew that if she were Nicole, she'd be deeply disappointed.

At the bottom of the page Ms. Black had indicated that she was leaving copies of the full script in the drama club office and that rehearsals would begin the next day. So at the end of classes, Mollie picked up her copy and headed for the meeting with her French teacher. Mrs. Preston lectured her for what seemed like days on how important it was to pay attention in class, and she reinforced the message with an extra dose of homework. But Mollie hardly noticed. She'd been walking on air all afternoon.

When dinnertime came, Mollie could hardly wait until her father began his daily ritual to spring her good news. "What did you do in school today, Nicole?" he asked as he passed the dishes around for seconds. He folded his arms across his chest and looked at his eldest daughter with a proud twinkle in his sharp blue eyes.

"Nothing much, Dad. I had a hassle with our yearbook photographer over the pictures of the football team. I wanted them standing in the shape of a V for Vista, but he insisted on the same old standard group shot."

"You, Cindy?"

"You know, Dad, same old thing. I nearly barfed on the food they served us for lunch. . . . I had a great time at water polo practice. . . . Oh yeah, and I got an A on my biology test."

"That's wonderful!" Mr. and Mrs. Lewis said in unison. They were unaccustomed to getting good grade reports from Cindy, who tended to study only when the surf wasn't up.

"Aw, it was easy. It was on fish," she said,

scooping up the last bite of chicken from her plate. Cindy was fascinated with marine life, and recently she'd started giving serious thought to becoming a marine biologist.

While Mrs. Lewis disappeared into the kitchen, Mr. Lewis turned to his youngest daughter. "And what about my baby? School treating you okay, Mollie?"

"Not bad," she said with unusual understatement. "I got the lead in the next school musical. It's called—"

The rest of her words were drowned out by a chorus of "For she's a jolly good fellow." And then her mother came back from the kitchen holding a carrot cake with "Congratulations, Mollie" written on top. Mollie just beamed.

"How did you know?" she demanded when the singing quieted down.

"I called Mom the minute I saw the list," Nicole told her.

"And it's all over school," Cindy added. "In fact, a couple of kids asked if I was the one who'd be playing Sandy. They didn't even know I had a kid sister. But they will soon." She gave Mollie a wink.

Suddenly Mollie felt overwhelmed. "I hope I won't let you down," she said seriously. "I've never done a musical before."

"Getting modest on us all of a sudden?" Cindy teased.

"You'll do fine, Mollie," her father said. "You're not the first Lewis to sing before a crowd, you know. Your mom had the lead in her senior class play."

"Robert, that's so long ago I'd almost forgotten!" Mrs. Lewis said with a grin. "But I had a great time. I remember that."

"Don't tell us you played Sandy, too," Nicole said.

"Oh, no. *Grease* came out long after I'd given up my acting career—for the good of mankind I should say. No, I was Daisy Mae in *Li'l Abner*."

"Really?" Cindy's eyebrows shot up like rockets. "I thought she was supposed to be sexy."

"Cindy!" Mr. Lewis scolded.

"Well, my hair was longer then," Mrs. Lewis said, "and I have to admit I was slimmer. . . ."

"Mom made a great Daisy Mae," Mollie put in. "Her yearbook said she gave an exciting, memorable performance—especially because of what she put in the Kickapoo joy juice."

Mrs. Lewis looked at her with a mixture of curiosity and embarrassment. "How did you know that?"

"Well, I found your yearbook in the attic one day, and I was interested in seeing what you looked like back then, and one thing led to another, and—"

"Mom, what's Kickapoo joy juice?" Cindy interrupted.

"Something like a love potion, as I recall."

"But what did you put in it?" Cindy pressed.

"Yellow food coloring," Mrs. Lewis replied. "I added it to the water as joke, to make everyone think it was whisky. Then when the guy who drank it on stage forgot his lines, the audience was convinced he was drunk. That's the thing about acting. It's only make-believe, but sometimes people take what they see as real."

"Great stunt. I've got to try it out sometime," Cindy said.

"Don't you dare," her mother said with a laugh.

"How come you're not still an actress, Mom?" Mollie asked.

Mrs. Lewis shook her head. "It just wasn't for me."

"I know what you mean," Cindy said. "My idea of fun is riding a wave, not standing on a stage smooching with a boy."

"Come on," Mollie said. "That's not what acting's all about."

"Are you sure you know what you're getting into?" Cindy shot back.

"What are you talking about?" Mollie demanded.

"I guess you didn't see the movie version of *Grease*," Cindy replied "There's this scene where John Travolta and Olivia Newton-John are on the beach kissing up a storm." She picked up a napkin and held it close to her heart. "Oh, Olivia, you mean so much to me." She kissed the napkin. "I can't live without you. I love you." She kissed the napkin again and again, making everyone at the table laugh.

"Maybe you should have tried out for this play," her father said.

That reminded Mollie of Nicole's audition, and

she turned to her sister. "I'm sorry you didn't get a part, too," she said. "You deserved it."

Nicole smiled. "Thanks, Mollie, but as I told you this morning, I'm really not interested."

"Not even when Mark's going to be in the play?" Cindy asked incredulously.

"It makes no difference," Nicole said stiffly.

"Then you've got to be the most generous person I know," Cindy went on. "You mean to tell me you really don't mind your sister kissing your boyfriend in front of everyone?"

Nicole nodded. "You heard what Mom said. It's just make-believe."

Mollie barely heard Nicole's reply, because it finally dawned on her what Cindy's teasing was all about. If the play was anything like the movie, then sometime soon she was going to have to stand up in front of her sisters, her parents, and the whole school and kiss Mark Russell.

"Uh, will you excuse me?" she asked nervously. "I've got to check something in my room." She rose from her chair and hurried up the steps to her bedroom at the end of the narrow hallway. Then she flopped down on her unmade bed and pored through the script she'd picked up that afternoon. Quickly she saw that Cindy had exaggerated and the musical wasn't nearly as hot as she'd implied. But Cindy hadn't been joking about the kissing! Near the end of Act Two Mollie came across a play note that made her heart lurch. *They kiss again, Danny getting more aggressive and passionate as the kiss goes on.*

Mollie groaned. With that one line she saw her triumph turning into a disaster. The moment she tried to play the scene, everyone would know her deepest secret. Mollie Lewis had never kissed a boy in her life.

Chapter 2

"*D*ahling, you look *mah-velous.*"

Mollie recognized Heather's throaty voice as she entered the auditorium the following day after school. There were half a dozen kids lolling around the stage, and Heather was giving a once-over look to the most gorgeous boy Mollie had seen in her life.

He had the type of looks people think of when they imagine the typical California boy: sun-bleached, slightly shaggy blond hair, tanned skin, bulging muscles, and sapphire-blue eyes—and all this with a face that'd fit in well with the gallery of movie and rock-star pinups on Mollie's bedroom wall. Even his voice was perfect, she noted as he told Heather, "You look marvelous, too, pumpkin," and swept her off her feet in an exaggerated, theatrical hug.

The two of them giggled as they parted, and as Mollie continued her walk down the auditorium aisle, she wondered who this boy was and how she could get to know him. Then the obvious dawned on her. He was a member of the cast, and for the next several weeks she'd be spending every day after school with him. She couldn't believe her good luck.

Heather was the first to notice her. "Hey, I remember you from yesterday. You sure you're ready to join this bunch of loonies?"

Mollie gave her a friendly smile. "You don't look crazy to me."

"That's 'cause you don't know her yet," the boy said. Extending his hand he helped her onto the stage. "By the way, I'm Kenny Slater. Ought to be easy to remember. I'm playing Kenickie." He patted the folded script jammed into the back pocket of his black drawstring pants.

"Pleased to meet you," Mollie said, surprised she could get the words out. She still felt a tingle in her hand where they'd touched. "I'm Mollie Lewis—alias Sandy."

"Our star!" Heather said. "Come on over and pull up some stage. If I know Ms. Black, we'll be here awhile before things get started."

"Is she always late?" Mollie asked.

Heather nodded. "Her drama class never begins on time either," she said, dangling her purple-stockinged legs over the stage apron.

"Yeah, she gets her kicks making grand entrances," Kenny added.

"I wouldn't know," Mollie said. "I wanted to take drama this year, but they stuck me in Lloyd's speech class instead."

Heather looked at her sympathetically. "We've all been there," she said. "But if you think Lloyd's a character, wait till you meet Black. She's the classic frustrated actress turned teacher." Heather directed her green eyes at Kenny. "Could you give me a rub right here?" She indicated the back of her neck. "I made the mistake of actually doing sit-ups during PE this afternoon." She patted her ample midsection. "Not that it's going to do me any good."

Obediently, Kenny began massaging Heather's neck. "Ooh, that's great," she said, sighing. "Mollie, this guy gives the best neck rubs in Santa Barbara. If you ever need one—"

"Hey, who said you could offer my services?" he asked with a grin that showed off dimples the size of the Grand Canyon. Then he gave Mollie a searching look. "Hmm! On second thought, I don't mind."

Mollie gave him a hundred-watt smile. She was rapidly developing a crush on Kenny and by the look in his eye she had a feeling it was mutual. Even so, she was too unsure of herself to answer him directly. Besides it wasn't clear where he stood with Heather. They were definitely friendly, but somehow she sensed they weren't a couple. "Uh, have you two known each other long?" she asked, hoping the question didn't sound too obvious.

Heather let out a laugh. "Too long! I can't stand the guy, but he won't go away."

Kenny nodded. "It's true. Heather and I have been fighting since sandbox days, but we're never apart for long." He rolled his eyes upward.

Heather spotted the look of utter confusion on Mollie's face and took pity on her. "Maybe I ought to explain," she said. "I guess you could say Kenny and I are the heart of the drama club. We've been in productions together forever. We're the ones who try out for everything—even those deep dramas nobody bothers to come see. But we have a lot of fun." She smiled. "Think you can take being with us?"

Mollie smiled back. "Are you kidding? I can't wait. This is like a dream come true for me."

"Spoken like a real trouper," Kenny said. "Let me introduce you to some of the gang." He pointed to a reedy boy with oversized glasses reading his script on the edge of the stage. "That's Jeff Marciano. We call him Marshmallow, 'cause he looks like such a softie, but on stage the guy's a Superman."

"Just call me Clark Kent." Jeff flicked his hand in a salute and continued to read.

"Those girls cackling in the corner are Helen, Marie, Maggie, and Emma," Kenny went on. "The two R's, Rick and Rob, are those jerks eyeing you from the front row."

"Quite a crew," Mollie said.

"There's more to come," Heather told her. "But the others are smart enough to know Black's gonna show up late. Of course, once she gets here, we'll be going into high gear."

"I hope I can keep up," Mollie said frankly.

"Don't worry. Black's kind of flaky, but she knows her stuff. She wouldn't pick a freshman like you if you weren't good," Kenny said.

"Thanks." Mollie was grateful for the compliment. "How did you kow I was a freshman?"

Kenny shrugged. "I haven't seen you around before."

"And, believe me, he looks," Heather added, with a wink of a heavily mascaraed eye.

"Hi, everyone!" Mark shouted his greeting as he ran down the center aisle and vaulted onto the stage.

Heather gave her a long look. "You know Mark?" she asked.

Mollie shrugged. "He's my sister's boyfriend."

Heather leaned her head back, and a look of revelation crossed her face. "I should have figured this out. You're Cindy and Nicole Lewis's sister."

"Yeah, you know them?"

"Only by reputation—the surfer and the super student." Heather smiled. "Well, it's nice that you already know your leading man. I think it's hard if the the guy's a total stranger, especially when it comes to the romantic scenes."

Mollie felt the blood drain from her face. Why did Heather have to remind her about that? She'd been feeling great until now, but all of a sudden she wanted to run and hide.

Heather sensed her uneasiness. "Did I say something wrong?" she asked.

"No," Mollie said, flicking her fingers through her hair with a practiced air of indifference. She had to steer the conversation away from that dreaded kiss. "So tell me about Ms. Black's acting career," she said casually.

"There's not much to tell. She thought she'd get her big break by auditioning for that soap, *Santa Barbara*. She figured she had an edge, living here and all. But she never made it past the first reading. So she's been pouring her soul into us ever since."

The auditorium door slammed open. "Don't look now, but here she comes," Mark said.

With the purposeful stride of a woman on a mission, Ms Black approached the group. To Mollie, she looked more like a student than a teacher, dressed in an oversized floral print shirt over a contrasting skirt, hot-pink patterned tights, black flats, and a matching black leather vest. Under her arm she carried a thick portfolio, which she threw onto one of the front-row seats. "Let's begin," she said abruptly.

Ms. Black's clipped, no-nonsense tone struck fear in Mollie's heart. For the first time since she'd entered the room, she remembered that there was going to be a lot of work involved in this show. It would be nothing like the plays she'd performed for her parents and friends when she was little, or her starring role as Nancy Hanks in the junior high President's Day Assembly—or even

like the talent show at the Y last summer. This
was the big time.

"All right, everyone, get out your scripts and sit
down on stage," Ms. Black said, pacing back and
forth in front of the first line of seats. "Today,
we're going to do a run-through. No singing. No
dancing. No movement. This is your chance to
get to know one another and the characters you'll
be portraying. One word of caution: as Miss Wynn-
Sommers will attest," she looked pointedly at
Heather, "I can be either as rough as Attila the
Hun or as gentle as Glinda the Good. So how can
you make sure I'll stay my sweet, kind self,
Heather?"

In a singsong voice Heather recited, "Always be
on time and know your lines. No drinking, no
smoking, and no bad-mouthing fellow cast members."

From the way she said it, Mollie had the feeling
that this was standard operating procedure for all
of Ms. Black's plays. At least these were rules
she'd have no trouble following.

"That's right," Ms. Black nodded her approval.
"Okay, before we begin, I want to remind you
we'll have rehearsals every afternoon at three
sharp. Set-construction and costume crews will
meet at seven P.M. Now, is everybody ready to
start?"

There was a collective mumble of yesses.

Ms. Black put her hand to her ear. "I'm sorry. I
didn't hear you. I said, are you ready?"

"Yes," the group said louder.

"I still can't hear you!"

"Yes, Ms. Black!" This time the shout was so loud the room resonated with the echo.

Mollie opened her script. She was sitting cross-legged right next to Kenny, and if it hadn't been for her excitement about the show, she didn't think she would have been able to stand being so close to him without falling to pieces. As it was, she was grateful she'd worn her jeans. At least she didn't have to worry about keeping a dress from riding up her legs on the hard stage floor.

As she began to read her lines, she found herself slipping away from the concerns of Mollie Lewis and into the role of Sandy. Since Ms. Black let them read without interruption, she had no idea if she was interpreting the lines correctly, but at the moment it didn't matter. She saw that while there was a lot of work ahead, there was also going to be a lot of fun. She couldn't wait until the next day, when the real rehearsals would begin.

After the run-through was over, Mollie dawdled a while, rummaging through her large canvas shoulder bag as if she were hunting for something. Actually she was biding her time, hoping to get a few moments alone with Kenny so she could ask him for a ride home. It didn't matter that she'd ridden her bike to school that day. She'd find a way to pick it up later. Nothing would stop her from trying to make this boy notice her.

But Kenny did a disappearing act on her. He was there when she began her bag search, but by the time she looked up again, he was on his way out the door with Ms. Black. For a second she thought about running after him; then she rejected that as too obvious—an eighth-grade tactic not befitting the freshman she was now.

Disappointed but not downcast, she turned to Heather, who was still gathering her own things together. "I thought it went well today," she said.

"Typical first-day run-through," Heather replied, slinging a purple book bag over her shoulder. "Well, I've got to go—got a hot date with my chemistry homework." She started down the aisle, then turned back. "Say, you going to join the set-construction crew?"

Mollie looked doubtful. "I don't think so."

"Don't let the word construction scare you off. It's not hard at all. Even a dumb clown like Kenny can do it."

Mollie's ears perked up. If Kenny was going to be there, she'd have to reconsider. "As a matter of fact, my dad once showed me how to use a hammer, she told Heather. "I'll think about it."

"No big hurry. The first meeting's tomorrow, but the actual building won't start for a day or two. Come when you can—if you want," Heather said. "Well, see ya."

Mollie was pretending to mull it over, but already she'd made up her mind. If Kenny Slater was going to be there, she would be, too.

Chapter 3

"*I feel like a lemming,*" Cindy said, scrunching up her pixielike nose.

"What's that?" her friend, Anna asked as they moved forward another inch in the cafeteria line.

"Miss Harris talked about them in biology this morning. They're these dum creatures who blindly follow each other into mass suicide—which is how I feel waiting for this food."

Anna stopped scanning the lunchtime crowd streaming through the door and faced her friend. "Your mother's a caterer, so how come she doesn't send you off to school with gourmet lunches?"

"I've been asking myself that question for years!" Cindy shook her head. "I guess she'd rather give us the responsibility of making or buying our own." The line began to move, and she reached over the stainless steel divider and scooped up a bowl of cottage cheese and pineapples. "No way I'm going to eat that hot stuff," she said, indicating a container of indefinable lumpy beige goo. "So, anything exciting happen this morning?"

"Nada." Anna sighed. "The year's already wound down to a dull, predictable routine."

"Sounds like you've got a case of the same blahs I've got," Cindy said. "Grant's home sick today, and that just makes it worse."

To Cindy's obvious horror, Anna took a helping of the goo. "I'm so bored I'm even willing to experiment with this stuff. I *think* it's chicken à la king." She looked down briefly before heaving another sigh. "Listen, my eyes have been glued to that door ever since we came in here, and I haven't seen a single boy I'd care to daydream about. Sad, isn't it?"

Cindy knew what she meant. Anna's crush on their mutual friend Duffy Duncan had fizzled out that past weekend after a less-than-successful date. She took a carton of milk. Then she reached into her red leather bag for some money and paid the cashier. "We've got to do something about this, Anna," she said. She led the way to a table near the window and set her tray down resolutely. "We've got to make some excitement."

Anna glanced at the poster on the far wall. "Maybe we should join the booster club."

Cindy's friend and water polo teammate Carey slid into the seat next to her. "What, and hang out with Katrina Martindale and her snobby crowd? Why?"

"Anna and I were just talking about how boring things are around here," Cindy said. "I'm not desperate enough to join the booster club, but we've got to do something...." Then she snapped her fingers. "I've got a great idea: it's time for the first annual Cindy Lewis Let's Get Crazy party!"

Anna leaned closer, resting her chin on her hands. "Okay, I'll bite. What's that?"

"A party that everyone will talk about for the rest of the year! We'll invite everyone," Cindy said, making it up as she spoke.

"Your parents are going to let you have another party after the last one?" Carey asked. She answered her own question with a shake of her thick blond hair.

Several weeks earlier—the night before their parents were due back from a vacation—Cindy and Nicole had thrown a party that had ended in a food fight, not to mention a marathon clean-up session.

"Oh, they won't mind, as long as they're around to keep an eye on things," Cindy told them. "Grant and I could host it together—our first party! Maybe get a band. Mom can supply the food—"

"I thought she didn't do stuff like that for you," Anna interrupted her to say.

"She only won't make lunch. But she'd love to help put this together; I'm sure of it. I suppose it'll mean I'll have to invite my sisters, but I can live with that. Oh, we can decorate the whole downstairs." Cindy's voice bubbled with enthusiasm.

"This is great—the shot in the arm every one of us needs. Can I count you two in?"

"For a party? Do you have to ask twice?" Anna said.

"Just name the date. I'll be there," Carey seconded.

The commotion at their table did not go unnoticed. Across the room, Sarah put down her tuna sandwich and nudged Mollie with her elbow. "What's with your sister?" she asked.

Mollie stretched her neck to see. "Don't know. Maybe she's reliving her date with Grant."

"Must have been pretty exciting," Linda said.

"I guess so," Mollie answered vaguely. She really didn't know what either of her sisters did on their dates beyond where and with whom they went. Even though she'd carefully cultivated an outward image of sophistication, she still felt very naive when it came to dating. She cleared her throat. "Ah, speaking of exciting dates ... if I get my way, I'll have one any day now."

"Oooh, I smell a scheme!" Sarah's dark eyes narrowed. "You going to tell us who the lucky boy is?"

"Kenny Slater." Just saying his name made Mollie's heart flutter.

"Who's he?" Sarah and Linda asked in unison.

"He's a senior and he's in *Grease* with me, and he's the most fantastic boy ever. I think he likes me, too. We talked a little before yesterday's rehearsal."

"Lucky girl," Linda said with obvious envy. "All

the boys on the newspaper staff are either taken, not worth having, or won't give me the time of day."

"You could always try another activity," Mollie said.

"Or another diet," Linda said, looking at Mollie's half-eaten container of blueberry yogurt.

"Tell me about it," Mollie said.

"You're not fat," Sarah objected. "And obviously your shape didn't keep this Kenny guy from paying attention to you."

"That's because when I'm with a guy, I forget about what I look like and concentrate on him," Mollie said, repeating something she'd read in *Young Miss*.

"I'll have to remember that," Linda said. "But at least you get to practice having a boyfriend in the play."

"You got any heavy kissing scenes?" Sarah prodded.

"A few," Mollie said lightly. But inside, the sensation of dread began to creep up again. What was she going to do when it came to THAT KISS?

"How do you feel about it?" Linda asked curiously.

"It's just make-believe," Mollie replied, tossing off the words as if they were as light as feathers. She couldn't admit the truth to her friends; they looked to her as *the* expert on dating and boys. Neither one had figured out yet that everything she knew came from magazines and movies, and she wasn't about to make that confession now.

The problem of how to deal with the kiss was still the number-one item in her mind when she went to rehearsal that afternoon. She sat in a front-row seat, her head buried in the script, trying her best not to make eye contact with Mark. She knew they'd never get to the kissing scene that afternoon, but just looking at him was a reminder of what was yet to come.

She wasn't alone for long. Heather dropped into the seat to her right and poked a finger over the script. "Nervous, huh?" she said between snaps of her bubble gum.

Mollie gave her a friendly smile. "A little."

"The first time's always the hardest. But don't worry about your lines today. Black's not expecting you to have them memorized."

"Oh, I'm not worried about that," Mollie said earnestly. It's ..." The words died in her throat. She couldn't even bear to tell this relative stranger about her kissing fear. "It's the singing," she finished lamely. "I've never sung on stage before." While this was true, Mollie *could* carry a tune, and she wasn't really that nervous about singing for an audience. But she knew it would make sense to someone like Heather.

"Mollie, this is musical comedy, not grand opera. All you have to do is look cute and you'll pull it off."

"Thanks," Mollie said, daring to look around. "Well, I guess we're about to find out. There's Ms. Black."

While they'd been talking, the drama coach had

arrived and was now pacing around the stage, making notes on a large legal pad. A few minutes later she called everyone to join her. "Let's get started. We're going to block out the first scene," she said briskly. "Heather, Helen. Enter stage right and stop here." She indicated a spot near the center of the stage. "The rest of you, stand backstage and await your cues."

Mollie's entry was near the end of the scene, so she sat down on a stool and watched the others in action. This was definitely different from the other productions she'd been in. She thought the two girls were already in top form as they slipped easily into the bubbly innocence of 1950s teens. She couldn't imagine how they could be better, but Ms. Black stopped them after the few lines.

"Heather, take out that chewing gum," she ordered.

"But Ms. Black, in the script it says Jan chews gum," Heather protested.

"Not in my version," the drama coach barked. "And Helen, I want you to glide when you walk. You think you're the greatest person in the world."

"She does, too," Kenny whispered in Mollie's ear.

Mollie felt a tingling vibration down to her toes. She hadn't realized he was standing so close.

Kenny pushed up the sleeves of his brown crewneck sweater. "I found out the hard way," he went on. "I dated her once."

Mollie was torn between giving him all her attention and concentrating on what was going on in the play. Splitting the difference, she spoke while staring ahead at the stage. "Do you feel funny about playing her boyfriend now?"

"Nah, we're still friends," he said. "Ooops, I'm on any second now. See you later—uh, Mollie, isn't it?"

He remembered my name! she thought happily, and watched entranced as he bounded on stage.

"Was he hitting on you?" Jeff asked, approaching from the curtain area where he'd been inspecting the ropes. "Got to watch out for those Henways."

Mollie gave him a puzzled look. "What's a Henway?"

"About three pounds," he said, laughing at his own joke.

Mollie groaned and poked him in the ribs with her script. "I should have expected as much from a boy wearing a Calvin Coolidge for President T-shirt," she said. "Are you always this funny?"

"It's the way I was born," he answered seriously. "Hey, if people are going to laugh at me, I'd just as soon it was because of what I say, not because of how I look."

Mollie inspected Jeff's face. With his prominent nose, he did look a little like a moose with floppy hair, but he wasn't all *that* bad. "You can try your jokes on me anytime," she said, trying to be friendly.

"Really? Thanks!" The genuine astonishment in his voice surprised her. "And as for Kenny, I'm serious about him. He loves playing with fire."

With a flick of his wrist he waved good-bye and sauntered on stage to deliver his line exactly on cue—leaving Mollie to fret over his last remark.

What had he meant by "playing with fire"? Shaking her head, she devoted her full attention to Kenny, now bantering with Jeff. Kenny's character was supposed to be a tough, egotistical, leather-jacket type. Kenny put a swagger into his walk and deepened his voice, and Mollie soon forgot everything else. She was too busy falling in love.

The next thing she knew, another deep voice— this time a female one—was bellowing from the audience. "Mollie! Mollie, where are you?"

Mollie shook herself to attention. Looking out at the stage, she saw the cast looking back at her with anticipation. She'd missed her cue! Embarrassed, she hopped off the stool and scuttled onto the stage. "Here I am," she said sheepishly.

A few of the cast members snickered, and Ms. Black, her hands on her hips, bored into her like a high-speed drill. "Mollie," she began, "I usually don't cast freshmen in these plays. But I made an exception in your case, because you appeared to have talent, enthusiasm, and a love for the theater—all qualities that most freshmen don't have. Now I'm seeing a trait that most people in your class *do* have: irresponsibility. From now on, I expect you to make your entrance on time. You're here to act, not jabber backstage with the boys. Am I making myself clear?"

Mollie stared at the stage floor. "Yes, Ms. Black,"

she said with unaccustomed meekness. "It won't happen again. I promise."

Ms. Black looked down at her script. "Now, where were we?"

"I was making my entrance—"

Ms. Black cut her short. "I know, I know." "Let's take it from Jan's line. Heather?"

The rest of the rehearsal passed without incident. Once Mollie got on stage she had fun with her character, finding the role easy to play. Sandy reminded her a little of Nicole—friendly, sweet, not a touch of malice in her heart. Mollie told herself to remember that. If she could keep Nicole in mind every time she went on stage she'd be a hit.

As rehearsal broke up, Mark and Mollie ended up walking out of the auditorium together. "I thought you were great today," he told her.

"I didn't exactly get off to a great start."

"You made up for it—that's for sure. Where'd you learn to act?"

"I had some lessons at the Y, but mostly it's just me," she said.

"Natural talent, huh?" he teased. "Well, I'm looking forward to our scenes together. Between us we'll knock 'em dead!"

"Right," Molly said, trying to imitate the confidence in his voice. But inside she was thinking, Easy for you to say. You're not the one who's going to be embarrassed in front of hundreds of people because you don't know how kiss!

When they reached the door to the parking lot,

Mark asked, "Need a ride home? I've got a bike rack, so it's no problem if you rode to school today."

Mollie was about to say yes, but suddenly she was struck by a better idea. "No, thanks," she said. "I've got an errand to run. I'll see you tomorrow."

Mollie ran outside to the corner bus stop. It was time for her to stop worrying about her problem and take some action.

Chapter 4

*M*ollie caught the first bus to Montecito, a small community a few miles north of Santa Barbara. She got off when she reached the town library and hurried inside. According to the clock, she only had half an hour before closing time. She'd have to work fast.

Wiping her brow on the sleeve of her black and white checked shirt, Mollie scanned the card catalogue under the letter K. She was looking for anything about kissing, but a quick search turned up only two books—one on a rock group, and a play called *K.I.S.S.—The Espionage Thriller*. Nothing else.

She looked up. The librarian was sitting alone behind the desk. A sign at her elbow read "Just ask. I can help you with anything from A to Z."

Anything but this! Mollie said to herself. The

middle-aged blond librarian looked too much like her mother. Then she spotted the *Reader's Guide to Periodical Literature*. Maybe a magazine would have what she wanted! She tore through the latest index and was rewarded with six articles on the art of kissing. Hurriedly, she filled out the request slips and presented them to the desk clerk. It was twenty minutes before closing. If she was lucky she'd have just enough time to glean the information needed.

While she waited for the clerk to return, Mollie congratulated herself on her foresight in coming all the way to Montecito. If anyone else had told her they'd done what she was doing now, she'd have laughed herself silly. Information this personal had to be handled discreetly! If she'd tried the school or city library, she would have been bound to run into someone asking why she was there or even peering over her shoulder to check on what she was researching. She felt much more comfortable surrounded by strangers.

Ten minutes later she left the library, disappointed. Only four of the articles were available, and they didn't tell her anything she didn't already know. They dealt with philosophy and feelings, and featured interviews with people who had Ph.D's at the end of their names. None of them dealt with the simple mechanics of a kiss. Where did her lips go in relation to the boy's? Did she stick her tongue into his mouth? If so, where? Did she let him put his tongue into hers? How could she breathe and kiss at the same time?

Over and over these questions floated through her head during the bus ride home. What she didn't think about was the hour. By the time she'd picked up her bicycle at school and pedaled home, it was close to seven.

To her amazement, her mother scooped her into her arms and hugged her tightly, as if she hadn't seen her in a year. "Mollie, I'm so glad you're all right," she said in a voice husky with emotion. Then she held Mollie at arm's length and narrowed her eyes into slits. "Where have you been?" she demanded. "Your father and I were ready to call the police."

"Why, Mom?" Mollie asked innocently. "I've been at the library."

The rest of the family, hearing the commotion, came in from the dining room. "The library?" echoed Nicole. "I didn't think you knew what the word meant."

"Why didn't you call?" her father demanded.

"I was squeezed for time," Mollie replied. "Rehearsal ran late, and I had to get to the library before it closed."

"But it's open till nine tonight," Nicole said.

"I don't mean the Santa Barbara library. I went to Montecito."

"Montecito! What were you doing there?" Cindy asked curiously.

Mollie couldn't bear to reveal the truth, so she made up a story on the spot. "Mrs. Preston's being a real ogre," she said. "She gave me another special assignment due tomorrow. But the school library was closed by the time I got out of rehearsal, and I was pretty sure the town library wouldn't have what I needed. So I hopped on a bus to Montecito. I'm really sorry I forgot about the time."

"We called all your friends," her mother told her. "No one knew where you were, and with all the terrible things we've been reading in the news ..."

"I'm sorry I worried you," Mollie said contritely. "It'll never happen again."

"You're not getting off that lightly, Mollie," her mother retorted. "You're getting kitchen duty for the rest of the week."

"Oh, Mom!" Mollie groaned. Cleaning up the dinner dishes was one of her least favorite activities—a close second to making her bed—and her parents knew it.

"You can grab a bite and then start right now," her father said firmly.

After Mollie finished in the kitchen, she joined Cindy and her mother in the family room, where they were watching a TV movie. The story wasn't much, and she was just thinking about leaving when the hero and heroine began a gentle embrace. She watched carefully as the man's lips touched the woman's. This is exactly what I need—a visual aid, Mollie thought. She took special note of the woman, cocking her own head slightly to the side the way the woman did, as the couple continued to kiss.

Cindy noticed her sister's unusual posture. "What are you doing, squirt?"

Quickly, Mollie straightened her head. "Uh, it's an exercise Ms. Black wants me to do," she said, inventing quickly. "Neck stretches. Um, I think I'll finish up in my room."

She slunk up to her bedroom, and Winston followed behind, nearly knocking over her life-size stand-up photo of Wham!'s George Michael. This is ridiculous, she thought as she tossed aside her nightgown and fell onto her rumpled bed. I can't keep making up stories. Sensing her discomfort, Winston padded over and began licking her face.

"Stop it, boy," Mollie said, stifling a giggle. She held his head in her hands and looked at him. "What am I going to do? I'm supposed to be the expert on kissing. Even if I tell the truth, no one's going to believe I've never done it before. And I'm going to look like the fool of all time when that kissing scene comes up." She sighed. "I've got to find some way of practicing."

The dog whined sympathetically. Even his droopy brown eyes seemed to reflect his concern. Briefly Mollie thought about trying out her skills on Winston but quickly threw the idea out the window. She was desperate, but not *that* desperate.

But it gave her another idea. Rummaging through her closet she found her old Baby No Tears doll. She hadn't played with it for years, but she'd put up a big fuss when her mother had suggested getting rid of it. She'd known it would come in handy someday.

Retreating to her bed, she began to kiss the doll. At first she felt silly holding it up to her lips, but as she experimented with different positions and angles she began to relax. It got even better when she pretended the doll was Rob Lowe, John James, Corey Hart, or one of the other guys whose pinups decorated her room.

Maybe I've blown this whole kissing thing out of proportion, she thought. If I can do it with a doll, how much harder would it be with a boy? Not much, she concluded, and certainly a whole lot more fun!

She was still playing with the doll when Cindy peered into the room. "Hey, what are you doing?"

Mollie was so startled she flipped the doll into the air. "None of your business," she hissed. "What are you doing here anyway? Don't you have any respect for privacy?"

"The door was partway open," Cindy said, looking at her oddly. "I thought you stopped playing with dolls years ago."

"I'm practicing CPR for health class," she snapped back. "Any objections?"

Cindy was about to say something about Mollie's teachers giving her weird assignments, but it was obvious her sister was in no mood to be teased, so she held back. "Hey, no big deal," she said.

"Sorry," Mollie replied. And she meant it. She *was* sorry she had to keep making up fibs to hide her fear of kissing. Telling lies was getting to be like eating Reese's pieces—once she got started, she couldn't quit. "Anyway, is there something you wanted?"

"Actually, there is," Cindy said, moving a couple of sweaters and some jeans and sitting down in the armchair. "Do you know what's eating Nicole? She's been grumpy all evening."

Mollie thought for a moment. "I don't know," she said. "Tonight was my night to set the table. Maybe she's mad she had to cover for me."

Cindy shook her head. "I think she was upset even before that."

"Have you asked her what the problem is?"

"I haven't had the chance. She's been in her room since after dinner," Cindy said.

"Maybe she'll talk to me," Mollie said. "I'm going to see right now." Determinedly she marched across the hall to Nicole's corner bedroom and knocked on the closed door. "May I talk to you, Nicole?" she said.

"Entrez!" came the reply from inside.

Mollie always felt a rush of envy when she entered Nicole's streamlined, stylish room. Everything had its own place, and there was a neat, clean feel about the decor. At the same time, it wasn't sterile. The wall photos, map of France, and crocheted pillows gave the room a comfortable, homey, lived-in look.

Nicole was hunched over her open French book. "The one bad thing about being a senior is they give you tons of homework," she said. *"C'est très dommage!*

"Look, Nicole," Mollie blurted out, "I'm really

sorry I stuck you with setting the dinner table tonight. I'll make it up to you."

"You sure will!" Nicole smiled slyly. "You've got kitchen duty the rest of the week."

"Don't rub it in," Mollie said, perching carefully on Nicole's floral-patterned bedspread. "But does that mean you're not mad at me anymore?"

"I never was," Nicole said.

"But you were grumpy tonight. Cindy said so."

"I didn't know it showed," Nicole said lightly. "Actually, I was upset with Mark."

"You two had a fight?"

"No, not really. He wanted me to come watch your rehearsal tomorrow, and when I told him I couldn't make it he got mad. Then I got mad at his getting mad. But we ironed it out and I'm over it now."

"I'd like you to come, too," Mollie said.

"Maybe some other time," Nicole said stiffly. "You know I'm very busy."

From the sound of Nicole's voice, Mollie had the feeling her sister wasn't giving her the real reason. "If you're still upset about not getting a part, I can understand," she said.

Nicole turned back to her desk. "Look, I'd like to chat, but I really have to get this reading done."

"Sure," Mollie said, rising. She'd found out what she wanted anyway. Nicole wasn't mad at *her;* she was upset about not being in the show. Mollie could think of no other reason why she'd be so reluctant to go to the rehearsal.

Chapter 5

*O*peration Kenny had begun.

Phase One got off with a whimper, not the great big bang Mollie had anticipated. Following a lunchtime strategy session with Linda, Sarah, and another friend, Margie, Mollie decided to play hard to get. She was convinced it was the only way to go, having read a recent *Seventeen* article that said boys considered girls who acted aloof more sophisticated and desirable. Even though she looked older than her age, she still felt she needed all the help she could get in landing a senior boy.

So, before that afternoon's rehearsal got under way, Mollie chatted a little with two of the other cast members, Marie and Emma, deliberately turning her back on Kenny every time he passed by. She hoped he'd be intrigued by her lack of interest, but the plan didn't work too well. Emma thought Kenny was a jerk and told Mollie she was showing good judgment in staying out of his way. Kenny responded to her cold shoulder by totally ignoring her, not even giving her so much as a "hi."

As she pedaled back to her house afterward, Mollie realized she'd have to rethink her strategy. Obviously, aloof girls didn't appeal to Kenny. So, for Phase Two, she decided to take the opposite tactic and be just as nice to him as she could. Being just a little bit friendly had gotten him talking to her the first day of rehearsal. All she had to do was be more obvious about it, and soon he'd be inviting her out on a date.

By the time Mollie parked her bike in the garage, her mind was made up. She'd begin Phase Two right away—at the set-construction meeting later that evening. But first she had to get through dinner.

To make up for her disappearing act the night before, she headed straight for the kitchen. She was setting the table when Nicole came home. "I'm in here," Mollie called when she heard the door slam.

Nicole was unzipping her jacket as she walked into the dining room. "You're exactly the person I want to see," she said angrily. "I made a fool out of myself because of you."

Mollie stared at her, completely baffled. "What are you talking about? What happened?"

"That's what I want to know. After French class today I asked Mrs. Preston why she was dumping all this extra work on you. And do you know what she told me?"

Mollie felt her face reddening. She hadn't meant for Nicole to take her so literally. "What?" she asked meekly.

"She said she hadn't given you *any* homework yesterday," Nicole continued, "let alone an assignment that required a special trip to the library. What's more, she looked at me as if I were some kind of wild-eyed idiot. I've never felt so humiliated in my life."

Mollie wanted to kick herself. Why, out of all her teachers, had she had to tell a fib about the one she and Nicole had in common? "I'm sorry, Nicole," she said contritely. "I lied about the French assignment, but I really did go to the library yesterday. I just can't tell you why."

"Why not?" Nicole demanded. "Are you in some kind of trouble?"

"Oh, no," Mollie cried. "It's got something to do with the show, and I'd rather not go into details— that's all."

"Mollie, what's happened to you? You've never kept secrets from me before." Nicole looked hurt.

Mollie felt so guilty she almost broke down and told her sister about her fear of kissing. But she couldn't get the words past her tongue. "I'm sorry, Nicole. I can't tell you. I just can't," she said at last. "But I never meant to get you in trouble with Preston. You've got to believe that." Her blue eyes pleaded with Nicole for forgiveness.

Nicole shook her head. "I don't understand why

you won't tell me the truth. But if you change your mind, you know where to find me," she said. Then she went upstairs to her room.

Slowly Mollie finished the table. She felt bad about hurting her sister's feelings. But nothing could keep her down for long, and by the time dinner was over and she'd put the last dish in the dishwasher, her usual high spirits were back. She ran up to her room, tore off the white jumpsuit she'd worn that day, and donned her newest acquisition—a V-neck, black knit minidress, which she accented with pink tights and short black boots. She pushed her hair back on one side with two pink barrettes and splashed on a heavenly cologne whose ad promised total satisfaction.

"Kenny Slater, here I come," she chirped happily to her reflection in the mirrored closet door. She couldn't see why her mother had told her she was too young to wear black. She thought the dress accented all her best features and made her look at least sixteen. But just to make sure her parents didn't ask questions, she tossed on her raincoat over the outfit.

She found her mother in the family room. "Mom, could you drive me to school?"she asked. "I've got a set-construction meeting tonight."

Her mother looked up from a sheaf of papers, a frown crossing her face. "I wish I'd known earlier, dear. I can't. I'm expecting a very important call any minute now from one of my clients."

Mollie shrugged. "That's okay. I'll ask Dad."

"He's not here," Mrs. Lewis said. "He went back

to the office right after dinner. Ask Nicole to take you. And I want you back here by nine-thirty. Understand?"

"Yes, Mom."

Nicole was on the phone when Mollie stuck her head through her bedroom door. *"Pssst.* Nicole," she whispered.

Nicole looked up, annoyed. "Can't you see I'm on the phone," she hissed.

"It's important."

Nicole sighed. To Mollie a chipped fingernail was grounds for declaring a state of emergency. But she couldn't ignore the anxious look on her youngest sister's face. "Hold on, Bitsy," she said into the receiver. Then she covered the mouthpiece. "What do you want, Mollie?"

"I need a ride to school."

"I don't believe this," Nicole cried. "Can't this wait till morning?"

"I mean now—tonight. I'm working on the set-construction crew," Mollie explained.

"Ask Mom."

"She told me to ask you."

Nicole sighed again. She knew she was stuck. She told Bitsy she'd call her back later, then hung up the phone. "Come on," she growled, "let's get this over with."

As soon as they got into the family station wagon, Mollie opened her coat. "Whew, it was hot in there," she said.

For the first time, Nicole got a good look at her

sister's outfit. "You're wearing *that* to build sets? Did Mom see you?"

"No," Mollie said. "That's why I wore the coat. I knew she'd make me change." She fastened her seat belt. "Don't tell her, okay?"

"Wouldn't jeans and a sweatshirt be more comfortable?"

"*If* I were going to hammer nails," Mollie said mysteriously. "But I've got an ulterior motive."

Nicole glanced at her sideways. "Sounds like a boy to me. Who is it?"

"Not telling," Mollie said. "I think he likes me, but I'm not sure yet."

That didn't satisfy Nicole's curiosity. "Do I know him?" she persisted.

"Not telling," Mollie repeated.

Nicole rapped her fingers on the steering wheel. "You're getting to be a real mystery, Mollie," she complained, "and I'm not so sure I like the new you. I remember when you used to tell me everything."

"Don't take it personally. When I'm ready to tell the world, you'll be the first person to know. I promise."

Nicole sniffed. "I'll take that promise with a huge dose of salt, and I promise not to tell Mom what you're really up to. But you'd better get someone else to drive you home. Ask Mark. He'll be there."

"Sure," Mollie said. But if things went her way, it would be another boy who'd be driving her home.

* * *

It was supposed to be a work session, but the set shop had a definite party atmosphere when Mollie walked in. A large portable stereo was blasting out dance music. Heather and Rick were dancing around in the far corner. Hammers were adding their own rhythmic beat to the air, and the sound of friendly chatter topped off the festive din.

It took Mollie a moment to orient herself. The set shop was a large room behind the auditorium. On one side were floor-to-ceiling wooden dividers that housed the flats from previous performances. On the other side were shelves full of painting supplies and a large sink in a counter that stretched most of the length of the wall. Several boys, including Mark, were standing nearby, looking at sketches of the sets to be built.

Construction equipment was set up in the middle of the room. Kenny and Jeff were guiding a large piece of plywood across a table saw, and for a moment the screeching blade drowned out the music. Mollie waved hi as she walked across the room toward Heather and Rick. But Kenny was too busy to notice.

She tossed her bag on the counter next to several others. "Hi, gang," she said.

Mark joined the group. "Good to see you, Mollie," he said. "Did Nicole come with you?"

"No. I think she figured it was bad enough she had to drive me out here."

Mark looked crestfallen. "Anyway, I'm glad you're

here. We could use another pair of hands." Then Mollie took off her coat and he did a double take as he saw her outfit. "Uh, I guess you wouldn't be interested in repainting flats."

"Not really. I'm not very good with paints," she said apologetically. "I even flunked finger painting in nursery school."

"We'll have to find this girl something neat to do," Heather said, eyeing Mollie's minidress as well. She herself was wearing a more utilitarian outfit of baggy gray sweats, accented only by a purple sweatband across her spiky haircut.

"Uh, I thought I might be a carpenter's aide," Mollie said, "you know, making sure everybody's got enough nails and screws." Out of the corner of her eye she kept watch on Kenny, now resting the freshly cut board against a side wall.

"In that case, go talk to Jeff; he's in charge of the heavy construction," Mark told her.

Mollie's happiness rose a notch higher. So far everything was going her way. Quickly, she skipped over to Jeff and Kenny. "Evening, boys," she said with a big smile. "Mark told me you could use some help."

Kenny reached into his jeans pocket and pulled out some change. "Would you be a doll and get me a Coke?" he asked. "I'm parched."

Mollie didn't want to move. She could think of nothing more heavenly than taking in the gorgeous sight in front of her for the rest of the evening. Kenny was wearing a dark blue sleeveless T-shirt that showed off his broad shoulders and firm muscles. He, too, was wearing a sweat-band—a paisley scarf—and with the hair off his face, his blue eyes took on an ever greater intensity.

"Okay," she said, finding her voice at last.

"Me, too," Jeff added, fishing out a fistful of change. "A Dr. Pepper."

"Sure," Mollie said. Playing gofer wasn't her favorite role, but it would do for now. She ran down the hall to the bank of vending machines and came back with the drinks. Kenny's smile when she handed him the open can was the best reward she could have asked for.

He gulped down the drink in one long swig. "Thanks, Mollie," he said, winking. "You saved my life."

"Yeah, thanks," Jeff added, accenting his gratitude with a loud burp.

Kenny dropped his empty can into the trash bin. "C'mon, Marshmallow, let's get this show on the road." He picked up one end of another large piece of plywood and Jeff picked up the other, accidentally knocking it against the side of the saw before balancing it on the table.

"What are you making?" Mollie asked.

"Cubes," Kenny answered, leaning his muscular body across the board as he lined it up with the blade.

"What for?"

He grinned. "Gonna be part of your bedroom—when we get done, that is."

Jeff pulled out a tape measure and began marking lines with the pencil he'd stashed over his right ear. "I'll bet it won't be as nice as your real one," he said, giving her a theatrical wink and a leer.

"You'll never find out," Mollie retorted. Turning to Kenny, she asked, "Where'd you learn to work with wood?"

"From my dad," he answered. He continued to concentrate on the plywood, now lining up a straightedge against Jeff's pencil marks. "We've got a whole workshop in our garage."

"You must really like it."

"Yeah," he said, drawing a line against the straightedge. "I like working with my hands."

"Me too," Mollie said, not really sure what she meant.

Kenny looked up. "You're into woodwork?"

Responding to his startled look, she rose to the challenge. Cindy had won Grant by showing him she was his equal as a surfer, and Mollie had no reason to believe the tactic wouldn't work with Kenny. "Don't look so surprised," she said. "I may be small, but I've done my share of hammering."

"That's refreshing," he said. "Most girls I know don't like this sort of thing." He looked around the room. "See? You and Heather are the only girls here."

"Of course, she counts for two," Jeff said, sketching a large shape in the air. Mollie and Kenny glared at him, making him add, "Only kidding. Can't you tell when I'm joking?"

"No, Marshmallow, we can't," Kenny said, giving him a friendly bop on the head.

Jeff took a pratfall onto the floor and howled in mock pain.

Mollie wished he'd go away. She and Kenny had just been getting into a meaningful talk, and he'd spoiled it. She turned to Kenny. "Seeing Jeff's disabled, can I help you balance this board?" she asked sweetly.

"That's okay," he said. "When Jeff recovers from his agony, he'll take over. But after we get this one cut we'll be ready to make the first cube. You can help nail it."

"Great! I'll go get the nails while you saw," Mollie said brightly. But behind her enthusiasm was a gnawing fear. She wasn't all that good at hammering, and if she wasn't careful, Kenny would soon know it.

Over on the workbench was a large plastic tray containing assorted nails. As Mollie stared at it, wondering hopelessly which nails were for plywood, she was suddenly struck with an idea: She would "accidentally" drop the tray on the floor! The scenario unfolded in her head as clearly as if she were watching it on TV. She'd cry out and look helplessly at the mess before her. Kenny would see her plight and offer to help her clean up. While they knelt together on the floor, he'd be drawn to her, and by the time they'd finished he'd be so taken he'd ask her to join him for a bite at Taco Rio or maybe McConnell's. It was absolutely foolproof, she thought, delighted. She'd get Kenny and get out of actually having to do any nailing.

With her back to the bench, Mollie slowly inched

the tray out over the edge of the counter. Then she turned and, pretending to reach for something up on the shelf, gave the tray a final nudge. With a satisfying crash it hit the floor, scattering hundreds of nails in a big circle.

"Oh, no!" Mollie cried loudly. She put her hands to her cheeks and rolled her eyes with convincing dismay.

There was only one problem: just as the tray fell, Kenny had put the plywood to the saw, and between the noise of the blade and the intensity of his concentration, he'd missed the entire performance.

Mollie was so annoyed she stamped her foot. That was a mistake. The nails rolled beneath her boot, she lost her balance, and before she could catch herself she went sprawling. Luckily she landed on a relatively bare patch of floor! But even so, her palm was grazed where she'd broken her fall, the heel of her tights had ripped, and the seat of her brand-new minidress was now covered with dust and wood shavings. Mollie's face burned with embarrassment. Not only had her plan failed dismally, but she'd made a fool of herself as well.

"You look as if you could use some help," a voice behind her said.

Hoping wildly, Mollie spun around. But it wasn't Kenny. It was Mark.

"Sorting out this mess could take you all night if you did it by yourself," he said.

Quickly, Mollie glanced toward the middle of

the room. Kenny was moving the boards off the saw. Would he ever turn around? she wondered. And would he come to her rescue if Mark were helping her? "Thanks, but you really don't have to bother," she said firmly. "I can handle it alone." To prove her point, she scooped up a handful of nails and dropped them into the tray.

"No, you can't." Mark took a nail back out of the tray. "See, you stuck this tenpenny in the sixteen-penny bin. You can't let them get all mixed up."

"Oh." Mollie had been too wrapped up with Kenny to pay close attention. She knew Mark was right. She needed help—and not just with the nails. Sneaking another peek at Kenny, she was dismayed to see him working away as if she'd never been there at all. She'd have to devise another strategy—and fast! And so Phase Three came into being.

Mollie concluded she'd made herself *too* available by hanging on to Kenny's every word. The key lay in splitting the difference between Phase One and Phase Two. She'd act nice to Kenny, but she'd try to arouse his jealousy, too. If Kenny saw her laughing and talking with Mark, maybe he'd see he wasn't the only boy in her life, and he'd take a deeper interest in her. The best part about this plan was that Mark was absolutely safe. She'd no sooner consider making a real play for him than she would shaving her head.

Having made her decision she turned away from Kenny and went back to sorting the nails with new determination. "Why do they have to make these things in so many sizes?" she wondered aloud.

"Nails are like people," Mark answered, holding up a long, thin one. "Here's Magic Johnson." He dropped it into the tray. "And there's Barney Rubble." He picked up a short flat-headed stud nail.

Mollie giggled. "Here's me and Nicole and Cindy," she said, lining up a small, medium, and large nail in a row.

Mark smiled. "Speaking of Nicole, Mollie, what do you think of our good news?"

"What good news?"

"Didn't she tell you? We're both going to go to UCLA next fall."

Mollie looked puzzled. "Uh-uh. The last time I heard, she hadn't made up her mind where she was going."

"Yeah, well, at first she had this funny idea about going to some school back east. Do you realize what kind of phone bills we'd run up talking over three thousand miles?"

While Mark was talking, Mollie sneaked another glance at Kenny. It was worth her while. She saw him looking at her, but she turned away before they actually made eye contact. Let him be interested in *her* for a change. She smiled at Mark, vaguely aware that he'd asked her a question. "I'm sorry," she said. "What'd you say?"

"I was talking about college."

"I can't wait till college," Mollie bubbled. "I'm definitely going east. Like New York City, maybe."

"Why?"

"So I can be as far away from my parents as possible."

"That's not always such a good thing," Mark said bitterly. He stopped throwing nails into the tray and tucked his arms close to his side.

Mollie was sorry she'd opened her big mouth. She'd just remembered that Nicole had told her Mark's parents were divorced. His father lived in Colorado or one of the other rectangular states—she didn't remember which one—and Mark hardly ever got to see him. "I shouldn't have said that," Mollie told him. "I mean, my folks are really good people, and lots of times I enjoy hanging out with them. But then they go and spoil it all by making up a bunch of dumb rules. I mean, yesterday my mom gave me kitchen duty 'cause I went to the library."

That got Mark's attention. "She has something against books?"

"No ... it's really sort of complicated and I don't want to get into it," Mollie hedged. "Let's drop the subject, okay? Why don't you tell me about some of the drama club's past performances, instead?"

Mark was a good storyteller, and some of his anecdotes about previous productions were very funny. Mollie laughed easily and teased Mark about his self-confessed bloopers, but all the while she was conscious of Kenny's movements, aware that he kept glancing her way.

When all the nails were finally back in the tray,

Mark pulled Mollie to her feet. "That's done!" he said with relief. "What do you say we go catch a bite to eat? It's too late to start in on something else."

Mollie glanced at her watch and pretended to consider, but actually she was taking the opportunity to check on Kenny again. He was nailing together one of those cubes with Jeff, and she let her eyes linger on him, willing him to turn around. Then suddenly he *did* look her way, so she smiled up at Mark and said in a clear voice, "I'd love to, Mark. I'm not very hungry, but I could sure go for a milkshake."

She picked up her raincoat and purse, and as they said good-bye to the other kids, Mollie noticed with great satisfaction that the look on Kenny's face was anything but indifferent. She'd gotten his attention at last, and now all she had to do was keep it.

Mark drove her to Casa de Burger, a popular fast-food restaurant not far from school. He got a Pepsi and a large order of fries, and Mollie asked for a small chocolate shake. It wasn't strictly on her diet, but she felt she deserved a treat to celebrate the success of Phase Three, and surely one measly little shake didn't count as cheating. . . .

As they sat in the booth, enjoying their food, talk turned—predictably—to Nicole.

"Are you disappointed she's not in the play?" Mollie asked.

Mark took a sip from his Pepsi. "I have to admit I *did* daydream about her and me playing the leads," he replied. "Not that I'm not happy you got the part, but to be honest, it would have been more fun with her."

"No offense taken," Mollie said, helping herself to one of his french fries.

"Here's what I don't understand," Mark went on. "I've asked her to come to rehearsals. I've even asked her to help out with set construction. But she keeps turning me down."

"I'm not surprised," Mollie told him. "Nicole's really disappointed about not being in the show."

"Really?" Mark said, surprised.

"She's trying to hide it. But I can tell. See, that's the difference between us. She tends to keep things to herself. Me, I let the world know everything. My life's an open book." *Except when it comes to boys,* she neglected to add.

As she drained the last swallow of her shake, Mollie caught sight of the wall clock. "Uh-oh, it's almost nine-thirty. My mom's going to kill me!" she said.

Mark took her home right away, and as they drove through the quiet streets, Mollie asked him about the people in the drama club. Her goal was to learn more about Kenny, but she didn't want to come right out and say she was interested. So she asked first about Heather and Jeff and a couple of the other kids. Unfortunately, she played it a little too safe, and by the time she mentioned Kenny's name, they'd reached her front door.

Oh, well, she thought blithely as she waved good-bye to Mark. I can always find out all about him myself—on our first date!

Chapter 6

As usual, Mollie overslept on Saturday morning. And by the time she padded down to the kitchen, everyone had beaten her to the breakfast table, leaving her alone with a sinkful of dirty dishes to clean up. Grumpily she wished her family would use paper plates; it would certainly make her life easier. But at least the sight of all those dirty dishes had one positive effect: it put her off having a big, fattening breakfast.

She was finishing up a grapefruit half when her father bounded into the room. "How's my little actress this morning?" he asked. "Rehearsing today?"

"No. We get weekends off," she told him. "Where's Mom?"

"Catering a wedding. She left early. I've got work to do this morning, too, checking some construction sites. But I'll be back this afternoon if anyone calls."

" 'Bye, Daddy," she said.

After he left, the room took on an eerie silence. Mollie turned on the radio just to have company, but she hardly noticed what songs were playing. She was too busy thinking about Kenny.

Yesterday's rehearsal had been a total failure as far as he was concerned. She'd been having trouble with her first solo song, the one that recapped the relationship Sandy and Danny had had before the start of the play, and Ms. Black had coached her to think about someone she liked a lot as she was singing. Automatically she'd turned to Kenny, who happened to be standing next to Mark on the stage, and then Ms. Black had stopped her and specifically ordered her not to look at Mark. Sitting in the kitchen, Mollie felt herself blush again, realizing how close she'd come to letting the entire cast know about her feelings for Kenny.

Kenny himself still didn't know, or if he did he wasn't showing her. Sure, he'd given her a friendly hello before rehearsal and he'd even flirted a bit between scenes. But at the end of the afternoon he'd left alone, and Mollie had spent her entire Friday night on the phone with her friends trying to figure him out. It was driving her crazy, being so close and yet so far away from her goal.

She was just about to get started on the dishes when Cindy came through the kitchen, plugged into her Walkman as usual and carrying a basket of wash. She disappeared into the adjacent laundry room and promptly returned empty-handed to lean over the breakfast table. "Mol, remember how you said you'd do anything in the world for me if I took over your kitchen duty last night?" she said, flashing Mollie her prettiest smile. "Well, your lucky day is here. I've got a favor to ask."

More like an order, Mollie thought ruefully. She cast a wary eye toward the laundry room. "Don't tell me you want me to do the wash."

"Okay, I'll *write* it down," Cindy retorted. "See, Mom left me with the job, but I just got off the phone with Grant. The waves are kicking up a storm. Six feet at least. He's on his way over right now. So you've got to help me out."

"But the wash!" Mollie protested. "I haven't dared go near the machine since that day I put in too much detergent and flooded the entire room."

"Hey, the only way you're ever going to learn how to do it right is to practice," Cindy told her. "Think of it this way. I'm actually doing you a favor."

"Thanks a heap," Mollie grumbled.

"Mol, you're a dear," she said. "See you later."

Mollie stared at her grapefruit rind and heaved a big sigh. Dirty dishes and dirty clothes all on the same day. It just wasn't fair.

Having finished the laundry, she was pairing the last of her father's socks when Nicole peered into the room. "Is my white and blue rugby shirt in that pile? I want to wear it today."

Mollie pointed to several neatly folded shirts

atop the dryer. "Over there, I think. What are you doing?"

"Horseback riding." Nicole was still wearing a pajama top over jeans and leather boots. "Thanks a lot for—" She stopped abruptly as she unfolded the shirt. Pink blotches had mysteriously appeared over the once white stripes. "Mollie! What happened!" she shouted. "My shirt's ruined. Now what am I going to do?"

"Wear another shirt?" Mollie suggested meekly.

"Be quiet," Nicole ordered. "This is great, just great. Mark's on his way over and my favorite shirt's ruined!" She rummaged through the other clean clothes. "And just look at my underwear!" She held up several newly pink panties and bras. "What'd you do, wash all my clothes with this?" She shook Cindy's red cotton shirt in front of her sister's nose.

Mollie's eyes began to fill with tears. "It was the last thing in the basket. How was I to know it'd run?"

"Don't give me that crying routine," Nicole snapped. "I'm not in the mood today. Who told you to do the wash anyway?"

"Cindy. She asked me to do it as a favor."

"Some favor!" Nicole stormed out of the room, and Mollie was left alone again, feeling more sorry for herself than ever.

An hour later, wearing a plaid flannel shirt, Nicole was riding along a hill side trail with Mark, on horses they'd rented from a stable on the outskirts of town. From her vantage point atop a gentle palomino she was able to see all the way to the ocean, a view marred only by the oil rigs that dotted the Santa Barbara channel. The day was crisp, the sky bright blue, and the hills alive with the tiny purple flowers that bloomed this time of year. She'd forgotten all about her earlier spat with Mollie, too happy about being with Mark in this beautiful setting.

Right ahead of them the rocky climb opened out onto a flat, grassy stretch of ground. "Let's race," Mark called to her. "Last one to that oak over there's a dirty skunk."

"You're on!" Nicole said. She wasn't a very good rider, but she was always up for a challenge. "Ready, set, go!"

Neither of the two horses needed much encouragement to canter, but the race was no contest. Nicole eased up when the speed got to be too much for her to handle. Mark reached the tree well ahead of her and was already dismounting by the time she got there.

"Howdy, stinker," he greeted her with a drawl. Then he helped her off her horse and tied its reins to one of the oak's branches.

"Just call me Pepe LePhew." She laughed good-naturedly. "Whew, that was some ride. I didn't realize you meant a real race."

"Um, I guess I never told you I used to take riding lessons when I was a kid."

"No, you never did," Nicole said, combing out her straight dark hair with her fingers. She loved the feeling of wind flowing through her hair, but she hated having to deal with the tangles. "I wanted a horse when I was little, but my parents wouldn't let me have one. They gave me Cindy and Mollie instead."

They sat down under the tree, Nicole resting her head on Mark's shoulder. "You could be a good horsewoman with a little practice. We'll have to do this more often."

"I'm game," she said. "Maybe next time we'll remember to bring some food with us. This would be a great place to have a picnic."

"It would also be great for other things." Mark bent down and gave her a kiss.

"Mmm, we *will* have to do this more often."

They sat for a minute in companionable silence, then Mark said. "I've been doing some research. There're some great trails in the Santa Monica Mountains, too."

"That's a pretty long drive just to go horseback riding—especially when it's so pretty up here."

"I don't mean now." Mark stroked her cheek with the back of his fingers. "I'm talking about next year, when we're at UCLA."

Nicole sat up straight. "You're not going to start on that kick again, are you? I told you, I'm still not sure where I want to go."

"I thought I'd talked you into UCLA. You know you'll be accepted there," Mark said.

"I'm still applying to other schools, too," Nicole said firmly. "Some of the colleges back east might be harder to get into, but I figure it's worth a try."

"You mean you're not going to make up your mind till you've heard from all of them?"

"What's the hurry? I wouldn't feel good about locking myself into UCLA before I knew what my options were."

"Even if you knew I was going to be there?" Mark sounded hurt.

Nicole turned to him and smiled. "That has nothing to do with us." She curled against his chest again and took his hand in hers. "Hey, I forgot to tell you. Bitsy's father is letting her take the boat out tomorrow. We're invited to go along."

"Great," he said. But he sounded distracted and a moment later he said irritably. "What's so special about eastern schools anyway? If you ask me, they're overrated."

The conversation was starting to irritate Nicole. "Why are we talking about this?" she demanded, pulling away. "All I'm doing is applying to a few schools that have great French programs. What's wrong with that?"

"You could study French in L.A., too."

"What's so special about L.A.?" Nicole got to her feet. "It's got too many people, too much smog, too much traffic."

"And beaches, good weather, plenty of museums, concerts, and all those other great things you like," Mark got up, too.

"But it's not the only place that does! There's a big world out there, and maybe I'd like to see what life's like outside California!"

"Why?"

"If you don't know the answer to that question, there's no point in continuing this conversation." Eyes flaring, Nicole swung up into her saddle and tried to turn her horse. But she went nowhere.

"You can't leave without untying that," Mark said flatly, pointing to the reins, still wrapped around the branch.

Blushing furiously, Nicole hopped down and began to untie the straps. But Mark pressed his hands over hers. "What are we doing?" he said. "Do you realize we're having a fight about school?"

Nicole sighed, her anger fading rapidly. "It *is* silly, isn't it?" She let go of the reins.

Mark moved closer. "Our first fight," he whispered. "I'm sorry, Nicole."

She smiled. "I'm sorry, too."

The only good thing is that now we get to kiss and make up." Lifting her chin up with his fingers he gave her a gentle kiss on the lips.

Responding warmly, Nicole wrapped her arms around him and showed him that a few words spoken in anger weren't going to spoil the day for her. Yet for the remainder of their date Nicole felt uneasy. It wasn't that Mark said anything else to make her upset. But now that they'd had a fight she realized they were not the perfect couple she'd believed them to be. How could a guy as sweet and guileless as Mark make her so angry and upset? The thought was unnerving, and she was almost relieved when he took her home.

As soon as Nicole closed the front door behind Mark, she came face to face with Mollie. Her younger sister was red-eyed, as if she'd been crying. "Have you been waiting for me?" Nicole asked.

Mollie nodded miserably. "I'm really sorry I ruined your shirt, Nicole. I promise I'll buy you another one."

Nicole took her arm. "That's okay. You don't have to. It was an honest mistake. Besides, maybe Mom will know how to bleach out the pink."

"You think so?" Mollie brightened. "But anyway, I'm sorry it happened, and I hope it didn't spoil your date."

"No, it was fine," Nicole said, sitting down on the steps. Cinders the cat leaped into her lap and she stroked his soft gray fur. She didn't say anything more, because she didn't feel like going into the details of her fight with Mark.

Mollie leaned against the banister. She felt enormously relieved not to be in her sister's doghouse any longer. Still, Nicole looked sad, and she wanted to say something to cheer her up. She thought of a surefire subject. "I think it's great that you and Mark are going to the same school next year," she said.

Nicole's chin lifted defiantly. "Did he tell you that?"

"Yeah. At rehearsal the other night," Mollie replied. "So, are you two going to get into the same dorm too? I think that'd be so romantic."

"Don't be silly!" Nicole said sharply, her earlier anger returning. "I haven't made up my mind what college to go to—let alone which dorm to live in!"

"Oh, maybe I heard wrong," Mollie said. She noted the frostiness in Nicole's voice and decided to switch to a safer subject. "By the way, when are you going to check out one of our rehearsals?"

"When I have some time," Nicole answered.

"Well, I think you'd better find some soon," Mollie told her. "Mark's pretty upset you haven't come by so far. I think he feels neglected."

"He has no reason to," Nicole said, rising. "And if you have any sense you'll stay out of our relationship. Okay?"

"Sure," Mollie said, watching helplessly as Nicole raced up the steps to her room. Then she sank to the floor, her elbows resting on her knees, and stared straight ahead, her mind in total confusion. She didn't know what she was doing or why it was happening. But it seemed that every time she made a move these days, Nicole got mad at her.

Chapter 7

*M*ollie had hoped that Nicole's bad mood would disappear overnight. But for the next few days, her sister seemed to be in a perpetual state of grumpiness. On Sunday night she refused to help Mollie with her lines, saying she wasn't in the mood. Mollie chalked it up to Nicole's disappointment about not being in the show, but she decided that all in all, it would be better to stay out of her sister's hair for a while. Considering the play was taking up more and more of her time, that wasn't too difficult. Unfortunately, things weren't much easier for her at rehearsals. Kenny's behavior continued to perplex her. On Monday he was all business and hardly said a word to her. On Tuesday Mollie managed to corral him into a conversation and felt she was making progress, but she was cut short when Ms. Black ar-

72

rived unusually early. Feeling frustrated, Mollie had a hard time keeping her lines straight. I've got to concentrate, she told herself firmly. But it was difficult paying attention to Kenny and to her acting at the same time, and by Thursday she was beginning to feel desperate.

'How far do you think we'll get today?" Mollie asked Heather as they studied their lines before rehearsal.

"Let's see." Heather thumbed through her well-worn copy of the script. "We're in Act Two. Looks like we'll make it to your big scene with Mark."

Mollie's heart sank. The day of the kiss had finally arrived. And even though she wasn't quite as obsessed about it as she'd been the week before, mostly because she'd diverted her energy to catching Kenny, the idea still filled her with dread.

"Mollie, what's wrong?" Heather looked at her with concern.

"Nothing. Why do you ask?" Mollie said, trying to sound casual.

"Does the expression 'white as a sheet' mean anything to you?" Then suddenly Heather understood. "You've never done a kissing scene before, have you?" she said.

Mollie looked at her sheepishly. "Well, they usually don't write them for fourteen-year-old girls."

"Oh, yeah, I forgot you were still a kid." Heather smiled. "But you must have done it for real. Work from your experience. That's what Black always says."

"I'll try," Mollie said quickly, eager to drop the subject.

"What are you two yakkity-yakkin' about? The latest shade of lipstick?" Kenny said, sliding into the seat next to Mollie's. For the past two days he'd been wearing his hair slicked back—"to get into the character," as he'd told them. Today he'd added a black leather jacket.

"You're probably as much an expert on that subject as we are," Heather retorted. "But if you really want to know, we were talking about drama. Mollie's nervous about her scene with Mark."

"The one where he puts the moves on you?" Kenny grinned slyly. "Hey, if you want to practice with me first—"

"She'd never stoop so low," Heather cut in.

Mollie wanted to shake her friend. It was *exactly* what she wanted to do, even though the invitation wasn't framed as sweetly as she'd have liked.

"Kenny, come over here," Rob, one of the other cast members, yelled. "We need you to settle a bet."

"Excuse me, girls." Kenny rose gracefully. "But remember, Mollie," he added with a wink, "the invitation's always open."

Heather watched with interest as Mollie followed Kenny with her eyes. "Don't listen to him. He's the biggest flirt at Vista," she said.

Mollie snapped her head back. "I couldn't care less," she said with a sniff. Her act seemed to fool

Heather, but inside she was exploding. Finally she had proof that Kenny liked her. He really liked her!

Seventy minutes and one act later, Mollie was on stage with Mark. In this scene they were supposed to be sitting far apart in the front seat of a car and then move slowly closer to each other. When Mollie first studied the scene she'd wondered how they were supposed to maneuver around the center console. Then she remembered that they didn't have bucket seats and center consoles back in the '50s. Now she stared ahead, wide-eyed with fear, as she waited for Ms. Black to give them the go-ahead.

Mollie had once read an article that said, "Never call fear, fear. Call it excitement. That will make the situation seem less scary." So she kept telling herself over and over that it was excitement she was feeling. But the silent chant didn't seem to help, and no matter what she called it, the feeling was horrible.

Ms. Black rapped a pencil on her chair for quiet. "In this scene your smoldering feelings for each other spark and light up," she said. "Until this point, you've been hiding them from your friends. Now that you're alone you can express them freely. It would be easy enough to let you go all lovey dovey, following what it says in the script. But I'd rather save that for the real performance. What I want to see now is facial expression, voice inflection, and body movement to show the same thing."

"Does that mean no kissing?" Mollie asked incredulously.

"Sorry to disappoint you. But yes," Ms. Black said with a rare smile. "If we practice this way, your kisses during the actual performances will be a lot fresher and look a lot more convincing."

Mollie wasn't sure of Ms. Black's logic, but she'd take a reprieve any way she could get it. She was so relieved she was positively lightheaded. Free of her terrible burden, at least for now, she was able to concentrate totally on her character and, as a result, gave her most convincing performance in days.

Her mood was infectious. Because she was relaxed, Mark was more comfortable, too. And Ms. Black let them play out the entire scene without a single interruption.

"Bravo," she cried, clapping her hands when they were done. Several others—including Heather and Kenny—joined in, and in the spirit of the moment Mollie leaped up and made a grand, sweeping bow. "Thank you. Thank you. Thank you," she said happily.

As she straightened up she looked out into the auditorium. There was a handful of students in the audience, but Mollie's glance rested on a slender, dark-haired girl who, at the moment, was slipping out the door. Mollie had been too preoccupied to notice her earlier. Now her mood darkened. Why was Nicole walking out on her?

*   *   *

When Cindy got home that afternoon she found Nicole sitting at the kitchen table doodling on a yellow legal pad. Peering over her sister's shoulder she said, "Is that your entry for this year's abstract art contest?"

Nicole looked up, as if she'd just snapped out of a trance. "Cindy, did you ever feel you had all the answers, only to find you've been asking all the wrong questions?"

"Constantly," Cindy replied. She sat down next to her sister. "You sound like your entire world's been shaken up. What's the problem?"

"It's probably not that serious, and I'm probably overreacting." She threw her hands into the air. "But I just don't know what's going on with me and Mark."

"You seem like the perfect couple to me. You lovebirds are always together."

"That's just the problem," Nicole said. "Mark's been on this togetherness kick lately, and instead of feeling good about it, I feel as if I want to run away from him. I don't understand it."

"Togetherness sounds good to me, sister. I wish Grant had more time to spend with me. Not that I'm complaining or anything. I mean, I'm still pretty new at this boyfriend–girlfriend stuff, but Grant sets aside part of every day for homework, and I can't get him to break the habit. I guess it's not too surprising, considering he's a professor's kid, but lately he's also been bugging *me* to study more. Can you believe it?"

Nicole didn't answer—she'd gone back to her

doodling—and Cindy was instantly contrite. "Sorry," she said. "We were talking about your problems, not mine. Go on, Nicole."

"Well, ever since I told Mark that I wasn't sure I wanted to go to the same college he does, he's been on my case. We had a fight about it the other day."

"Is that why you've been moping around doing your imitation of Winston?" Cindy let her lower lip droop in a hangdog pout. "It doesn't sound that serious to me."

"But yesterday he stuck a copy of that song 'I Love L.A.' in my locker!" Nicole said, sounding distressed.

"So?"

"So it's all part of his campaign to get me to change my mind and go to UCLA. He even told Mollie we were going together. Can you imagine? Next thing you know he'll be sending me guidebooks and city maps!"

"The guy's crazy about you." Cindy shrugged. "Maybe he just needs a little reassurance that you care about him, too."

Nicole nodded. "I've been trying to do just that. Mark was upset at me for not coming to his rehearsals. So I decided to stop in this afternoon and watch for a while, just to show him I cared. But as I was watching him do a scene with Mollie— she's really good, by the way—I realized I didn't want to be there."

"Why not?"

"Quite frankly, it wasn't any fun. It was sort of

like watching somebody put a jigsaw puzzle together—exciting for the person doing it, but not for the viewer. I felt out of place, so I left. But now I'm worried Mark's not going to understand."

"You going out with him tonight?" Cindy asked.

"No, he's still working on the sets."

"Why don't you go over there with him?"

"I'm no carpenter."

"If Mollie can do it, so can you."

"Mollie can't. Don't you remember her big speech at dinner the other night—about how hammers are incompatible with long fingernails? Besides, the only reason she went in the first place was to try to catch the eye of some guy."

"Oh, yeah? Who?"

"I don't know," Nicole replied. "For once in her life, Mollie's mouth is shut like a steel trap."

"Anyway, I still say go," Cindy insisted. "You won't know if you like it unless you try, and it'll give you a chance to show Mark you're part of his world."

Nicole took another look at her doodling. She knew from experience that she'd only feel worse if she sat around and brooded. "You're right," she said. "In fact, I think I'll go over to his house right now and see if we can grab a bite to eat together before we head for the school."

"Way to go, Nicole," Cindy said, patting her shoulder. "Uh, but before you leave, I've got something to ask. Do you know any guys who'd like to come to a positively great party?"

"Yours?" Nicole's eyebrows shot up. "I thought you had the guest list under control."

"There was a big screw-up. I thought Grant was going to invite all the guys, and he thought I was. So now I've got a houseful of girls coming—and only a handful of boys."

"Uh-oh," Nicole said. "What about your friends on the swim team?"

"It's too late. Most of them have already made plans," Cindy wailed. "Can you ask around? Please?"

Nicole hadn't heard Cindy sound so desperate since the time she accidentally rode her bike over their mother's newly planted herb garden. "Of course I will, Cindy," she said reassuringly.

Cindy's relief was visible. "Thanks, Nicole. You're the best."

"I'll ask Mark to see what he can do, too."

"Great! But whatever you do, don't invite any more girls. I've already told the shrimp the party is off limits to her girl friends."

"Okay," Nicole said, rising. "Tell Mom I'm eating out tonight, will you?"

"Gotcha."

Nicole was gone by the time Mollie got home from rehearsal. No one mentioned why, but Mollie didn't have to ask. She was convinced it was her fault, that somehow she'd made Nicole so upset at rehearsal that she'd decided to eat out rather than face her sister. The only trouble was, Mollie hadn't the foggiest idea what she'd done wrong.

Chapter 8

*M*ollie *believed in destiny, and as she stood* in the lunch line the following day, she felt it was ready to strike. For the first time since she'd known him, Kenny was sitting alone. It was an opportunity she couldn't ignore.

Balancing her tray in front of her, she eased between the tables until she was standing in front of him. At first he didn't notice her; his head was buried in a history textbook. Then she cleared her throat.

He looked up and smiled. "Hi, there."

"Uh, anybody sitting here?"

"The swarm hasn't arrived yet. Pull up a seat if you want."

"Thanks. Actually I've got something to ask you."

"Sure, as long as it's quick. I've got to cram for a test next period."

Mollie sat down, her stomach churning like the inside of a washing machine. She cleared her throat again. "Um, Kenny, my sister's having this big party tomorrow night. I'd like you to come, if you can." She bit her lip, hoping she didn't sound as if she were begging.

"Sounds like fun," he said, and Mollie nearly jumped for joy. She was all ready to thank the moon, the stars, Ms. Black, and even her parents for having moved to Santa Barbara in the first place, when he went on. "Jeannie and I are always up for a good party," he said, and Mollie felt her stomach go hollow.

"Uh, who's Jeannie?" she asked, hoping it was something silly, like the name of his car.

"My girl friend," he said matter-of-factly.

"G—girl friend?" Mollie didn't even try to hide her shock. She'd never seen him hanging out with any one girl, least of all one named Jeannie.

Kenny looked at her in surprise. "Yeah, You mean you didn't know?"

"How could I—"

"That's right. You're just a freshman. I suppose you've never seen her around." All of a sudden, he looked embarrassed, as it finally dawned on him why she'd offered the invitation. "Actually, I forgot we're supposed to be going out with one of Jeannie's friends. Sorry—"

"Uh, I just remembered something I've got to do," Mollie said, cutting him off before he could say anything more and standing up awkwardly. Her milk carton shook precariously, but even if it had spilled all over the floor she couldn't have felt more humiliated. All those hours of planning and scheming, all those days of staring at him with hopeful anticipation, had been a total waste!

"See ya at rehearsal," he said. He looked down at his book, equally embarrassed and obviously eager to finish the conversation.

Feeling as if she were wrapped in a fog, Mollie walked away from his table. She couldn't bear to sit with her friends right now, and she might have spent the entire period wandering aimlessly if Heather hadn't seen the look of utter despair on her face and stopped her.

"Mollie, come over here," she said, taking the tray from Mollie's numb arms and setting it next to hers on the table. "What's wrong? You look green. Did Mrs. Stockbriar make you sit through her entire collection of health films?"

"I'm an idiot, Heather," Mollie said.

"A typical freshman complaint," Heather noted.

Mollie's eyes filled with tears. "I'm serious."

Heather pulled a tissue from her purse. "Here, let it out," she said. "Whatever it is, you'll feel better if you talk about it."

Mollie took the tissue and pressed it against her eyes. Stubbornly, she vowed not to make a public scene, but her misery nearly overwhelmed her. "I've just made a total fool of myself," she said brokenly. "I asked Kenny to this party my sister's having, and he told me he's got a girl friend."

Heather patted her hand sympathetically. "I'm

sorry, Mollie. If I'd known you had a crush on him, I would have told you about Jeannie and saved you an awful lot of grief. But you did a pretty good job of keeping your feelings a secret."

"I thought he liked me. He's always talking to me at rehearsals," Mollie said almost defiantly.

"That's Kenny's style," Heather explained. "His girl friend goes to West Side, so he doesn't see anything wrong with flirting with every girl in *this* school. To him it's a harmless diversion. But obviously you took it to heart."

"How could I have been so stupid?"

"Hey, don't be so hard on yourself. You're not the only one."

Mollie dropped her tissue. "You, too?"

Heather nodded. "Kenny and I have been good friends forever. But last year we did this two-character play together, and I took the role too seriously and fell for him." She smiled ruefully. "Pretty dumb, huh, expecting a hunk like him to go for someone like me."

"What do you mean? There's nothing wrong with you."

"Take a good look at me, Mollie. No guy's gonna waste his time on the Pillsbury dough girl."

Mollie couldn't believe what she was hearing. True, Heather was overweight, but she was nowhere near the blimp she seemed to think she was. In fact, her sense of humor and friendly spirit had made more of an impression on Mollie than her dress size, and she told Heather so.

"You're the last person I'd figure for a weight complex," she said.

"Why do you think I took up acting? It's nice to pretend for a little while that I'm someone else," Heather said. "But I don't suppose you'd understand that. You've probably never had to diet in your life."

Mollie couldn't hold back a laugh. "Are you kidding? I gain five pounds just looking at a bowl of ice cream. If I didn't constantly diet I'd look—" She broke off abruptly, before she said something embarrassing.

"Like me? That's okay, Mollie. I know what I look like and I've more or less accepted it. I just wish I could find a guy who would." She turned away for a moment. "Good grief. Listen to me. Here you are, all shaken up, and I'm complaining to you. I'm sorry."

"No, that's okay. I think I'll survive," Mollie said, deliberately brushing aside her own troubles in sympathy for Heather. Then she had a great idea. "Listen, are you doing anything tomorrow evening? If you're free, I'd like you to come to Cindy's party. She's convinced it's going to be a night to remember."

"Are you sure?" Heather asked warily. "She doesn't really know me."

"But I do, and that's good enough," Mollie said firmly.

"Thanks, Mollie." Heather gave her a big smile. "I'd love to come."

"Party starts at seven-thirty," Mollie told her.

Then out of the corner of her eye she spotted Nicole and Mark sitting together. Nicole had left the house early that morning, so Mollie hadn't had a chance to ask her about her disappearing act of the day before. But she thought now might be a good time to raise the question. "Listen, Heather," she said. "I've got to go over and talk to my sister right now. But thanks a lot for the talk. You've really been a big help."

"You've been a big help, too," Heather said. "See you after school."

Mollie sauntered over to Nicole's table. "Got any room for a kid sister?" she asked.

"We're busy now," Nicole said curtly. "Maybe later, Mollie." Her voice was unusually tense, as if she were holding back her feelings.

By contrast, Mark gave her his usual friendly grin and moved over to offer her an empty seat. "No, sit down," he said. "We're all one big happy family, right?"

"Mark . . ." Nicole said warningly.

He ignored her. "So, Mollie, you all set for Cindy's party?"

"I suppose," Mollie said uncertainly. She felt as if she'd just walked into the twilight zone, with Mark as warm and welcome as a June afternoon and Nicole as cold and chilling as a winter snowstorm. "I just invited Heather, too."

"Uh-oh. Cindy's going to kill you," Mark said. "Didn't she tell you she's overloaded with girls? She ran up to me this morning and begged me to bring over every guy I know."

Too late Mollie remembered Cindy telling her not to ask any girl friends. Oh, this is just great, she brooded inwardly. Now I'm in hot water with both my sisters! But she said, "I don't see how one more's going to make a difference."

"I don't know," Mark said. "She seemed pretty desperate."

"It's her first party with Grant. She wants it to be perfect. I can understand that." Mollie hardly knew what she was saying. She was looking at Mark and talking to him, but her mind was focused on Nicole. Her sister seemed to want no part of this conversation, and Mollie had the sense that Nicole was sending her mental messages to go away. She couldn't remember ever feeling so unwanted.

"I was telling Nicole how well the show's coming together," Mark was saying. "Wouldn't you agree?"

"I don't want to talk about it," Mollie said, rising. "I just came by to say hi. I've, uh, got a test next period I've got to study for."

Between them, Nicole and Kenny had made her feel as appealing as moldy old leftovers.

She bolted from the cafeteria and made it to the girls' room before she lost control. Then she just let the tears fall, not caring that she was rapidly developing a bad case of raccoon eyes from dripping mascara.

This was the most disastrous lunchtime in the entire fourteen-and-a-quarter years of my life, she thought miserably. It was almost enough to make a girl swear off food forever.

Chapter 9

"*M*ollie! Mollie! Are you coming out or not?" Cindy banged on Mollie's bedroom door the following evening. "The party starts in an hour and I need help right now!"

"Okay, okay, stop shouting!" Mollie said, shouting back. She turned down her stereo and opened the door a crack, and Cindy saw that she was still wearing the blue romper she'd worn to the beach that afternoon.

"You're not dressed!" Cindy exclaimed, looking pointedly from her sister's beach clothes to her own black satin pants and wild floral blazer.

"I'm not coming down," Mollie grumbled through the crack.

"Listen, shrimp, I don't have time for jokes."

"I'm serious, Cindy. I don't want anything to do with your party."

"Since when? All week long you've been looking at me with puppy-dog eyes, begging to help out. Well, now your chance has come."

"I've changed my mind."

"Unchange it," Cindy urged. "I can't believe I'm actually saying this, but I need you. Grant just called. He's got a flat tire so he'll be late. And Mom and Daddy already left for dinner, and I still don't have all the decorations up. I'm sunk without you. I really am."

Feeling a strong little-sister sense of obligation, Mollie opened her door wide. "Okay, I'll help. But I'm still not coming to the party."

"We'll talk about it later," Cindy said. She was already halfway down the stairs.

Mollie followed her slowly. She still hadn't shaken the blahs that had descended on her like a heavy fog the day before. She'd thought a day at the beach with her friend Arlene would help, but it had only made her feel worse. Her friend had unwittingly ruined the afternoon with her gushing talk about her Friday-night date.

Mollie was delighted that Arlene had found a new boyfriend, but she wished *she'd* had some good news to report, too. Besides that, seeing Arlene brought back all the horrible emotions she'd felt when she learned she was the only one of her junior high group to be assigned to Vista. And she couldn't help thinking that if she'd gone to West Side with Arlene and the others, she never would've had to face the heartbreak of meeting Kenny.

In the end, Mollie couldn't bear to burst Arlene's balloon with her own sad story. But she couldn't stay and listen to Arlene's bragging either, so she made up an excuse about coming down with a cold and retreated home to her room.

Now she looked at what Cindy had done to the living room. The ceiling was decorated with red, white, and blue streamers, and the pictures on the walls had been replaced by sports and rock posters from Cindy's room. "I think it looks fine," she told her sister. "What else do you need?"

"I need you to help me take Mom's things out of here," Cindy replied.

Mollie nodded knowingly. The last time they'd had a party, a few of their mother's crystal animals had been rearranged by the rowdier-than-expected crowd. This time, with their parents coming back from dinner before the party was in full swing, there was little chance of anyone getting out of control. Even so, neither girl wanted to tempt fate.

When they'd finished stashing the breakables, Cindy got out a bag of balloons. "Here, help me blow these up," she ordered. "Then tell me why you don't want to come to the party."

"We need some music around here," Mollie said brightly, hoping the sound would block out all meaningful conversation between them. The last thing she wanted to do now was talk.

"Having second thoughts?" Cindy asked. She went to the family room and popped a dance tape into the cassette deck. When she returned, Mollie was holding out a balloon she'd blown up. "Why are you holding on to that one balloon?" Cindy asked.

"I can't seem to tie it," Mollie confessed.

"Oh, never mind. Give it to me."

Mollie tried to pass the balloon to her sister, but somehow she let go, and it whizzed around the room until Smokey pounced on it. "Maybe I'd better clear the zoo out of here," she said. "No one needs a cat for a dance partner."

Cindy reached for another balloon. "Good idea, shrimp. There may be a brain hiding in that head after all."

Scooping up the cats in her arms and herding Winston in front of her, Mollie took the pets out to the garage. On her return trip she went through the kitchen, where she saw Nicole bent over the oven, checking the status of the finger food their mother had helped Cindy make earlier in the day. "I didn't know you were here," Mollie exclaimed.

Nicole spun around. "Last time I checked I still lived here," she said. "Is that what you're wearing tonight?"

"My sisters the fashion experts," Mollie exclaimed. "I've already heard enough from Cindy."

"Aren't you touchy," Nicole retorted. She returned her attention to the baking sheet. "Did you come to help with the food?"

"No, I'm helping Cindy," Mollie said quickly, then paused, not knowing what else to say. One part of her was still angry at Nicole for being so mean to her the day before. The other part wanted to clear the air so that they could be friends again. But as long as she had such mixed feelings, maybe it was better to stay away from Nicole. Maybe time would help her oldest sister forget about the Mrs. Preston episode, the ruined shirt, the play, and everything else that was rubbing her the wrong way. "I'd better get back," Mollie said at last, and she went back to the living room.

Nicole shrugged and put another batch of cheese puffs in the oven. Mollie sure is acting strange these days, she thought. But she chalked it up to the pressures of the play, her relative newness to Vista, and just plain being fourteen years old. Under other circumstances Nicole would have liked to talk to her about it, but at the moment she was too caught up in her confusion over Mark.

Things had almost come to a head at lunch the day before, right after Mark told her he was taking her to Disneyland the following weekend. There was nothing wrong with that; she'd always had a good time when she'd been there. But she was upset with Mark's tone, the way he'd said it almost like an order, as if he expected her to agree immediately and be wild with gratitude.

But she wasn't. Her first thought was the time involved. It was a good three-hour drive each way and, added to the time at the park, it meant she'd be spending the entire day with him. Strangely, the thought made her uncomfortable.

So she told him she'd have to think about it, and Mark was dissatisfied with that answer, and before she knew it they were locked into another argument, like the one they'd had the day they'd gone horseback riding. It was only Mollie's unexpected arrival that had prevented it from developing into a full-blown fight.

Nicole wondered if she was crazy to feel so ungrateful for Mark's love. He'd probably push her again tonight, but she'd already resolved to keep things as light and carefree as possible. This was supposed to be a party, after all, and parties were for kicking back and talking nonsense, not serious stuff.

Meanwhile, in the family room, Mollie was arranging paper napkins on as many free surfaces as she could find. "This way no one's going to wipe their hands on the drapes," she told Cindy, shouting to be heard over the music.

"Won't you reconsider and come to the party?" Cindy shouted back. "I feel bad about you doing all this work for nothing."

"Consider it credit against all the favors I'll ask you to do in the future," Mollie said just as the doorbell rang.

"Oh, no, they're coming already!" Cindy fluffed up her hair and scooted to the door.

It was Grant, holding two large plastic bags. "I brought the ice," he said, kissing her on the nose. "You look saucy tonight. Ready to dance?" He swayed his hips in time to the music.

"Not with two ice bags," she said, taking them gingerly from his hands. Just then another boy walked through the open door. "Duffy!" she called happily.

The red-haired boy gave her a salute. "Captain Duffy at your command. I came early to see if I could help out."

"Good. Take these into the kitchen and see if Nicole needs a hand," she said, passing on the bags. "Grant, maybe you could help me move back the furniture so we have a dance floor."

Mollie watched them from the family room. The music, the smell of cooking, and the decorations had turned the downstairs into Party Central. Suddenly the idea of locking herself away in her room didn't seem so appealing. Quietly, she slipped back upstairs and changed into a more appropriate outfit. And by the time she'd brushed her hair, put on her makeup, and come back downstairs, the living room had filled with the first arrivals—girls outnumbering boys almost three to one.

Since she hadn't eaten dinner, Mollie slipped into the kitchen and grabbed several cheese puffs and a couple of stuffed mushrooms. When she came back out, Cindy was talking to someone at the door.

"Do I know you?" Mollie heard Cindy ask.

"I'm Heather Wynn-Sommers. You're Cindy Lewis, right?"

Cindy looked embarrassed. "I'm very sorry, but this party's by invitation only. You're going to—"

"I invited her." Mollie stepped forward, casting

a leave-her-alone look at Cindy. "Come on in, Heather. The party's just starting."

"She's not mad, is she?" Heather asked after she and Mollie were out of Cindy's earshot.

"Nah. She's just upset 'cause there are so many girls here. But we don't need boys to have a good time, right?"

"Speak for yourself, kid," Heather said with a wink.

Mollie wasn't sure whether or not she was joking. Heather looked dressed to kill in a loose-fitting cobalt-blue dress that deemphasized her figure. She wore long purple and blue drop-earrings and skillfully applied pink and purple shadow around her eyes, drawing attention to her most attractive feature. "Mark told me about the girl problem and asked me to invite Jeff. I know he's kind of geeky, but he's a boy." She looked around. "So where's the party? Or have I walked into a game of statues?"

"They're not warmed up yet," Mollie said almost apologetically. "Maybe we need a change of music. Something to get kids dancing." She led Heather to the family room, and they started sorting through the Lewises' collection of cassettes.

"Here, try this," Heather said, handing Mollie a tape.

Mollie popped it in the machine, and immediately Tina Turner's powerful, sultry voice filled the room. "That's more like it!" she said happily as kids started moving irresistibly to the beat.

Heather was moving, too, lip-synching to the

song in perfect imitation of Turner's dynamic style, and Mollie watched her, amazed. It was as if the singer had lent Heather her spirit for the evening, magically transforming her from a plump high-school girl into a fiery rock star.

Mollie wasn't the only one who'd noticed the transformation. Several other kids gathered around to watch, and when the song was over, one of the guys said, "Way to go, Tina! How about an encore?"

Heather laughed but willingly obliged, kicking off her shoes and picking up a bread stick to use as a microphone. She was even more convincing the second time around, and one by one the rest of the guests noticed what was going on and came over to join the fun.

When the song ended, Heather looked around and saw she'd captured everyone's attention. "Any-one else want to try?" she said, then took a bite out of her "microphone."

"Let's have a contest," Cindy called out. "Who wants to be next?"

"Me!" Duffy said immediately. "I'll do Prince."

Cindy found the right tape and put it into the machine, and Duffy started in. He didn't exactly keep to the beat, and halfway through he forgot the words he was supposed to be lip-synching, but he hammed it up so much that by the end everyone was roaring with laughter.

After that, Grant did a pretty good Bruce Springsteen, and then Mark spoke up. "Do you have 'I've Got You, Babe,' Cindy?" He grabbed

Nicole's hand and pulled her forward. "We're going to do a duet."

"We are?" Nicole's eyes widened in dismay. "But I can't sing."

"You don't have to. Just pretend you're Chrissie Hynde. C'mon."

"Yeah, c'mon, Nicole, you can do it," everyone around her said, urging her forward. Cindy searched through her cassette collection for the song and popped it into the machine. "Now, ladies and gentlemen," she announced, "I present our next act, the Vista virtuosos, Santa Barbara's own Nicole and Mark. Take it away, guys."

As the music started, Nicole suddenly understood why she'd been glad when she didn't get a part in *Grease*. There was something about standing in front of all her friends, pretending to be someone else, that made her feel as if she were taking off her clothes in public. Mark's choice of song didn't help ease her self-consciousness either. The lyrics were about holding hands, kissing good night, and staying together forever—things she and Mark never talked about. Yet here they were now, saying the words out loud, and she could tell from Mark's expression he wasn't just playing a part. He really meant what he was singing—or pretending to sing.

At the start of the act Nicole had been able to plaster a smile on her face. But as they reached the final chorus, the *I got you*'s got harder and harder to mouth, and the words felt as hollow as the lip-synching itself. Almost before the song faded out she slipped her hand from Mark's and disappeared into the kitchen.

Mark followed on her heel, trailed by a chorus of unappreciative boos. "You didn't give a very convincing performance out there," he complained. "What's wrong?"

"Nothing," she said. "I'm not a very good actress, that's all."

"I guess I should have asked you first."

"That would have been nice! You have to understand, Mark. I'm not cut out to perform like that in front of a bunch of people."

"I'm sorry," he said, taking her in his arms. He kissed the top of her head. "Let's stick to more mundane things—like dancing."

Nicole sighed uneasily. "Okay," she said at last.

They rejoined the party in time to see Mollie finish her rendition of a Cyndi Lauper song. The youngest Lewis was having a blast, prancing around the room like a five-foot firecracker, and at the end Jeff joined in the fun by picking her up and spinning her around his shoulders.

Mollie didn't know who it was at first, and for one glorious moment she had the crazy fantasy that Kenny had abandoned Jeannie, sneaked into the party, and made this grand gesture to show how much he cared. But her fantasy could've gone down in the *Guinness Book of World Records* as the briefest one ever, because the instant Jeff put her down, reality reared its ugly head.

As he let her go, Jeff gave her the most dejected look she'd seen since the time she'd forgotten to feed Winston. "What's wrong?" she asked.

"Nothing," he said with a shrug. "I'm mimicking your face."

She followed him as he eased through the crowd to an empty space in the family room. "I really look like that?" she asked, horrified.

"A good actor should always be aware of her facial expressions," he intoned. Then he reached into a nearby bowl of potato chips and shoved one into his mouth, holding it in place with his upper lip. "This is my imitation of a rabbit in bad need of a toothbrush."

"Silly boy," Mollie said, unable to hold back a giggle.

"I hope you didn't mind me stepping into your act back there. Sometimes I get these uncontrollable urges. Know what I mean?" He jerked his body around for a few seconds. "That was my impression of Ben Franklin after the lightning struck."

Mollie was really laughing now. "Are you always on like this?" she asked him.

"This is my party mode." He showed her the back of his neck, pointing to a spot to the right of his red-tipped ducktail. "Down here is the button for school." He touched his neck. "Yes, teacher, no, teacher, anything you say, teacher," he droned like a robot. "Somewhere back there's the normal mode, but I haven't found it yet."

Mollie grinned broadly, enjoying Jeff's antics. He was making her feel comfortable and helping her forget the troubling parts of her life. "I'm glad you came tonight," she said. "Lately, I haven't had much to laugh about."

"I'm sorry about that," he said seriously. "I felt bad when I heard about your misunderstanding with Kenny."

"Who told you?" Mollie snapped, fire erupting from her blue eyes.

"Kenny," he said matter-of-factly. "He's my best buddy. He tells me everything."

All of a sudden Mollie saw red. "So he sent you here on a mercy mission to make the poor little freshman feel better. Is that it? Well, you can forget it, bozo! I don't need charity." She stomped away in disgust. Why does everything good always turn into sawdust? she wondered bleakly.

"Wait!" Jeff called after her. "You've got it all wrong!" But Mollie didn't hear him.

Meanwhile Nicole and Mark were dancing together, while one of Cindy's friends mouthed a heartrending version of a Lionel Richie ballad. Midway through the song, Duffy tapped on Mark's shoulder. "My turn," he announced.

"Go away," Mark said grumpily. "She's mine."

"I know that, bud," Duffy said. "I'm not asking for her heart, just a dance."

"Can't you find someone else?"

"Don't I have any say in this?" Nicole asked.

"Would you rather dance with him than me?" Mark challenged.

"It's not an either/or choice," Nicole said. "I can dance with whom I want, when I want."

"So you'd rather dance with him," Mark said, his voice rising.

"Uh, I think I hear Cindy calling me," Duffy said awkwardly.

"Don't move, Duf," Nicole ordered. "Look, Mark, you know how much I like you, but you've been clinging to me like wet seaweed all night. I need some breathing room."

"So now I'm algae?" Mark exclaimed. "Maybe you want to fumigate the place."

"Don't be so literal," Nicole pleaded. "We'll have to talk about this, Mark, but now's not the time. Come on, Duffy, let's dance." Without daring to look at Mark, she led Duffy across the room.

"If that's what you want, two can play the game," Mark muttered. He stormed into the family room and walked straight into Mollie. "You're just the person I was looking for," he said. And without another word he led her back into the living room and held her close as they slow-danced to another oldie.

Mollie fell willingly into his hold. If neither of her sisters was available to console her, an older-brother type like Mark would do. She wished all boys could be like him: honest, up-front, sensitive. "Thanks, Mark," she told him, "I need this right now."

"Me, too," he said. As he swung her around, she caught a quick glimpse of Nicole, and then suddenly Mark pulled her toward him and kissed her. Not a stage kiss. Not a light brush of the lips. But a genuine, honest boy/girl kiss.

Mollie was stunned. It had happened so quickly she couldn't have done anything to prevent it even if she'd wanted to. And as it left her with a wonderful, tingling sensation, she wasn't sure she *would* have wanted to.

At that moment the song ended, and Mollie came to her senses and bolted up to her bedroom. She couldn't stay at the party one second longer. The kiss that she'd dreaded for so long had finally happened, and it changed everything. It felt natural, as if she'd known exactly how to do it all this time.

Most important, it felt good, and Mollie was very very scared of what might happen if Mark kissed her again.

Chapter 10

*T*he next morning Cindy barged into Mollie's room and pounced on her bed. "Wake up, Mollie," she said, shaking her sister vigorously.

Mollie refused to come out of her cocoon of blue checkerboard quilt. "What time is it?" she groaned.

"Nine-thirty," Cindy said cheerfully.

"Go away." Mollie covered her head. "Come back in ten years."

Cindy peeled down the quilt and leaned closer to her sister. "Mom wants us to clean up the mess downstairs—right now."

Slowly, Mollie sat up. She peered at Cindy through eyelashes half stuck together by the layer of mascara she'd neglected to remove the night before. "Why me? It was your party."

Cindy shrugged. "I can't do it alone."

"Get Nicole to help."

"Can't. She already left for Bitsy's house—for a heart-to-heart talk, I guess. You may not have heard, but she broke up with Mark last night."

The news jolted Mollie to attention, and the memory of Mark's kiss flooded her brain. Nicole must have seen it! "Did she tell you why they broke up?" she asked cautiously. She was afraid to hear the answer, but she knew she had to ask.

Cindy got up and walked over to Mollie's dresser from which she pulled out underwear, jogging shorts, and a T-shirt. "She said something about things not working out for them anymore. Who knows what that really means." She threw the clothes on Mollie's bed. "Here, put these on. I'll meet you downstairs."

After Cindy left, Mollie stared at the clothes as if they contained some mystical answer to her problems. She decided that Cindy was probably too embarrassed to say what she must have known—that Nicole had broken up with Mark because of that kiss. And she figured that Nicole had left the house early to avoid having to look at her and relive the pain all over again.

Slowly Mollie got dressed. She was *glad* Nicole wasn't around; she had no idea what she could possibly say to her sister.

A few minutes later she ventured downstairs and saw why her mother was in such a hurry for a cleanup. It looked as if the great California earthquake had finally struck. Streamers, rumpled-up napkins, paper cups, and empty soda cans littered the floor and furniture. The Lewises' entire cassette collection was scattered around the stereo. And the kitchen would probably be worse.

"Here, take one of these," Cindy ordered, pointing to a box of garden-size trash bags. "You hold. I'll toss."

"Nicole must have been really down in the dumps this morning," Mollie ventured, fishing for more information about the breakup.

"She wasn't her usual cheery self, that's for sure. It's got to be rough for her. She was so happy with Mark at first. But I guess nothing lasts forever."

Mollie sighed. "Was it a big scene?" she asked.

"Nah, I didn't even know till she told me this morning. By the way, thanks for inviting Heather. She sure got the party going. Where'd you find her?"

"She's in the show with me."

Cindy plunked several soda cans into the bag. "It's funny how we divide ourselves into groups. I must know every sweat at Vista, but if it weren't for you I never would've crossed paths with someone like Heather. She's all right."

Mollie nodded. "Too bad the boys are put off by her size. Why do they have to put so much emphasis on a girl's figure anyway?" She leaned against the sofa, finding the weight of the trash bag too much to deal with this early in the morning.

"Probably 'cause we let them," Cindy said. "I

think we put too much emphasis on boys, too. Sometimes they're just not worth it."

Mollie gulped. "Don't tell me you're having problems with Grant."

"Not really," Cindy said. "I just can't figure him out sometimes. We had lots of fun together last night, but when I suggested driving down to the beach this afternoon, he said he had to study." She shook her head. "Never thought I'd be competing with a textbook! Do yourself a favor, Mollie. Don't get involved with anyone."

Mollie couldn't tell her, but it was already too late. Last night's kiss had changed everything. Even though she didn't understand it and wasn't sure she wanted it, she was already involved— with Mark.

For once in her life Mollie was glad she had homework. She spent the whole afternoon catching up on all the studying she'd ignored for the past week. And that night she took her dinner up to her room, telling her parents she was cramming hard for an algebra test the next day. If they wondered why their youngest daughter was hitting the books without being forced to, they didn't mention it. Mollie figured they didn't want to tamper with success.

In truth the test wasn't until Wednesday, but studying equations was one way to block Nicole, Mark, and the rest of the human race out of her mind. By the time Mollie went to bed, she'd come up with the answers to enough "x equals what" problems to give her a permanent prejudice against the twenty-fourth letter of the alphabet. But it was only a temporary reprieve, and when Monday morning rolled around, she realized her day of hiding was over. Like it or not, she'd have to face the world.

Luckily, Mollie's morning teachers kept her very busy, so it wasn't until lunchtime that her thoughts returned to Nicole and Mark—and the kiss.

"Did you hear this one?" Linda said, trying to grab Mollie's attention. "Jeremy Clayton came up with a way to put some excitement into Mr. DeLeon's class."

Mollie was up for anything that would keep her mind off her troubles. "What'd he do? Pass around a copy of *Penthouse*?"

"Yccch!" Linda turned up her nose. "No, he set off a strip of caps. DeLeon went through the whole class asking everyone who did it. 'Course we didn't tell him, but he figured out it was Jeremy anyway and sent him off to see the principal. The best part was, it took up nearly the whole period!"

"I wish my morning had been as dramatic," Sarah chipped in. "The only thing noteworthy was seeing Brenda Savini with her braces off."

Linda swallowed a bite of her peanut butter and jelly sandwich. "Mollie, you haven't told us about your sister's party yet. Any fireworks there?"

The last thing Mollie wanted to do was talk about Saturday night. "You didn't miss much," she said as casually as possible. "I left early myself."

"And I'd heard the Lewises gave such great parties." Sarah sniffed.

Mollie knew her friends were still miffed that they hadn't been invited, and she was about to explain for the hundredth time that Cindy had forbidden her to ask anyone, when she saw something that made her quake all the way down to her short suede boots: Mark had just emerged from the cafeteria line, and he seemed to be heading her way.

Abruptly, Mollie dropped the frosted brownie she'd bought to cheer herself up and started gathering her belongings together.

"What's wrong?" Sarah asked. "You look as if you'd just seen a ghost."

"Uh—it's the brownie," Mollie said, improvising quickly. "Ever since I've been on this diet, rich desserts don't seem to agree with me." She smiled weakly. "I think I'd better get some fresh air."

Ignoring her friends' puzzled looks, she hurried to the side door and escaped into the sunny courtyard. Other students were outside, too, enjoying the blue sky and warm breezes of a spectacular autumn day. But it was wasted on Mollie, who was lost in a wash of bleak thoughts and stormy emotions.

What if Mark had stopped to talk with me? she thought desperately. What if he'd put his arm around me or flirted with me in front of my friends? I would have died! And yet the memory of his tingling kiss was very strong, and she felt herself drawn to him because of it.

Mollie sat down on a bench as far away from the other kids as possible and found she was breathing hard. She'd had a very narrow escape, but the next time she might not be so lucky. From now on she'd have to avoid the cafeteria during lunch hour, even if it meant getting up early to make sandwiches.

For a moment she pondered the possibilities of brown-bag lunches, and then a horrible thought hit her. She could avoid Mark in the cafeteria, but there was no way to avoid him at rehearsals. Unless a miracle occurred, every day between now and show time she'd have to see Mark and talk to him and play the role of his girl friend. There was no escaping that.

Chapter 11

*C*indy *didn't think anything was odd about* Mollie's asking to join her and Grant at the beach that afternoon. She'd heard on the radio that a big storm was brewing in Mexico. That always meant high waves along the entire southern California coast, and she'd daydreamed about the great surf all day. As far as she was concerned, the beach was the *only* place to go after school.

Mollie sat on a blanket and watched her sister and Grant zip through the surf. She knew she should feel guilty about missing rehearsal that afternoon. But she already felt awful enough, and there was only so much despair her brain could handle. She even rationalized that her absence was a good thing, because it would give her understudy, Julie Powers, a chance to practice the role.

Grant carried his surfboard onto the beach, water dripping from his black wetsuit. "It's great out here, Mollie. Want to take a ride with me?"

"Like this?" She pointed to her landlubbing outfit.

Grant shrugged. "It's only water."

"That's what I mean. It's wet. Some other day, maybe."

"Sure," Grant said easily. "In the meantime, watch this." He left his surfboard on his towel and waded into the water toward Cindy, just finishing a ride of her own. Then the two of them paddled out on her board, and to Mollie's amazement, Cindy climbed onto Grant's shoulders as the wave began to crest behind them. It was a trick she'd never seen them do before, and she held her breath till the ride was over and Cindy and Grant were safe in the shallows. Then she cheered and waved as her sister shot her fist into the air.

"Grant found out about a tandem surfing competition coming up next month, and he signed us up!" Cindy told her during their ride home later that afternoon. "Do you believe it?"

"You're always saying you want new challenges," Grant teased.

"I should have kept my big mouth shut. Do you know how scary it is standing six feet *over* the waves?"

Mollie listened with half an ear as they discussed tandem techniques and the quality of the day's surfing. And before she knew it, Grant was pulling his Trans Am into the Lewises' driveway.

"Okay, Mollie, here's where you get out," Cindy said.

"Aren't you coming in?"

Cindy slid her black sunglasses down the bridge of her nose. "Grant and I have some *personal* things to discuss."

The light went on in Mollie's brain. "Oh, right. In that case, I'll see you at dinner."

She closed the car door and steeled herself for the inevitable. Without Cindy there as a diversion, she'd have no choice but to face Nicole.

She waited for Grant to back out before crossing the driveway to the front door. That's why she didn't see the girl waiting for her on the steps until she'd cleared the hedge that bordered the walk.

"Heather!" she exclaimed. "What are you doing here?"

"We've got to talk." The red-haired girl looked very upset. "Mollie Lewis, you're in one big heap of trouble."

"What's wrong?" Mollie asked. "Was Ms. Black mad 'cause I didn't show up?"

Heather got up from the step. "That's putting it mildly," she said, brushing off the back of her pants. "Where in the blazes were you?"

Nervously, Mollie pulled a few leaves off the azalea bush. "Um. At the beach," she mumbled.

Heather looked at her aghast. "What's going on, Mollie? First you pull a vanishing act at the party.

Now this." She took Mollie's arm and led her to the sidewalk. "Come on, we're going for a walk," she said. "I want to get to the bottom of this."

Mollie went along sheepishly. She knew she'd have to face Nicole if she went inside, and at the moment even an angry Heather seemed like a better alternative.

"I'm miserable," she told Heather. "I've made a mess of everything I've done lately."

"Add today's rehearsal to the list," Heather said bluntly. "Black's furious. She said if you don't show up tomorrow you're out of the show."

"She can't do that!" Mollie exclaimed.

"This is the real world, Mollie. She can do anything she wants. So if you have any desire at all to play Sandy, you'd better show on time. And I'll tell you something else. Julie would love it if you bowed out. She's raring to take your place."

Mollie found the news unsettling. The show was the one positive thing left in her existence. If she lost that, she might as well stay in her room for the rest of her life. "I'll be there," she said softly. Somehow, she'd face Mark.

"Good." Heather patted her back. "Now, would you tell me what brought all this on? If you've got a problem I'd like to help."

They continued walking. Two houses down from the Lewises' was a topiary garden. Mollie had never gotten over her amazement at seeing animals carved out of shrubs, and when she was younger she had begged to ride on the make-believe horse. But now she passed by, too absorbed in her problems to notice.

"Nicole broke up with Mark," she said at last.

"So that's why he was down in the mouth today." Heather nodded knowingly.

"Did he say anything about me?" Mollie asked.

"No, he was off in his own little world." Heather looked at her quickly. "Why should he mention you?"

"He kissed me at the party. Didn't you see him?"

"No."

The event loomed so large in Mollie's life it surprised her to learn it hadn't sounded an alarm throughout the entire party. "Nicole saw it. I'm sure of that."

"What did you do? What happened?"

"I panicked and ran up to my room. The next day Cindy told me they broke up."

"How do you know it had anything to do with the kiss?"

"It had to. I've been doing an awful lot of thinking since then, and one thing I figured out is that Mark likes me. Ever since rehearsals started he's been awfully nice to me. At first I just thought he was doing the big-sister's-boyfriend routine. But then he held me real tight when we danced, and after that kiss . . ."

"But he and Nicole were so close," Heather protested. "And you said *she* broke up with him."

"Don't you see? That's because she caught him red-handed," Mollie insisted. "Nicole's usually a very even-tempered person, but if she feels she's been wronged, she can really let loose. She must have sensed something all along, 'cause lately she's been treating me like a cockroach."

"Have you talked to her about it?" Heather asked. "I mean, you're not in love with Mark, right?"

"I haven't had the guts to face her," Mollie admitted. "She's got to think I'm the most despicable thing on earth. And as for Mark ... I just don't know. I didn't think I liked him except as a friend, but after that kiss ..."

"It was *that* good?" Heather sounded doubtful.

"It felt super—unlike anything else," Mollie said dreamily.

"Better than any other boy's kiss?"

Mollie looked down at the cracks in the sidewalk. "Promise you won't tell anyone?" Heather nodded silently. "I've never been kissed before."

Heather was quiet for a few moments, then she said, "If you don't have anything to compare it with, how do you know it was that special?"

"It felt good," Mollie insisted.

"Did it ever occur to you that it's the kiss itself you're stuck on? That your first kiss from *any* boy would make you feel that way?"

"You think I'm making too much of it?"

"As I recall, Mark's not the guy you've been jumping through hoops to attract these past few weeks."

Mollie thought about it. What Heather said was

true; she'd never given Mark a second glance until now. "But he and Nicole broke up over me," she said doggedly. "That's got to mean something."

"It means you're overdue for a heart-to-heart with your sister," Heather said. "I'm not a big expert on relationships, but common sense tells me a couple as tight as those two wouldn't break up over one measly kiss."

Mollie put her hands in her pockets and turned back toward her house. Heather'd made her see things in a new light, but she still felt apprehensive. "So what do I say to Nicole?" she wondered aloud.

"What do you *want* to say?"

"That I want things to be back to normal with us."

"So tell her," Heather said simply.

"Easy enough for you to say," Mollie muttered.

"It *will* be easy—if it comes from your heart." Heather stopped and put a hand on Mollie's shoulder. "I've got to run. Go home and talk to her now, and let me know what happens, okay?"

Mollie stared at the house. "I don't even know if she's home yet. Maybe I'll just wait...."

"Mollie!" Heather glared at her.

Mollie looked sheepish. "You're right. I'll talk to her now," she said. "Thanks a lot, Heather. You've been a big help—I think."

Heather walked toward the bus stop at the bottom of the hill. "See you at rehearsal," she shouted when she was halfway down the block.

Mollie waved good-bye, still standing where Heather had left her. Then she slowly walked up the path to the front door. The time had come to settle things with Nicole—for better or worse.

Chapter 12

*C*losing the door lightly behind her, Mollie padded up the carpeted stairs. Nicole's door was wide open and her sister was sitting cross-legged on her bed, hunched over a yellow legal pad. Her long straight hair shielded her face from view, and Mollie almost chickened out and escaped to her own room. But her feet stuck to the floor like glue, as if they knew there was no turning back now.

She knocked on the wall tentatively. Startled, Nicole looked up from her writing but then, to Mollie's surprise, she smiled. *"Bonjour,"* she said. "Come on in, stranger."

Mollie thought it was a good sign that Nicole was using French words again—something she hadn't done for weeks. But still she was nervous.

"Uh, are you sure?" she asked haltingly. "I, uh, I don't want to keep you from your homework."

"It's not homework," Nicole said. She leaned back and placed the pad on her night table. "I'm writing down my thoughts about Mark. I broke up with him, you know."

Mollie didn't know what to make of Nicole's voice; her sister sounded sad but not heartbroken. She forced herself to press ahead. "Yeah, that's what I wanted to talk to you about. I'm really very sorry, Nicole."

"Thanks for caring," Nicole answered. "Come pull up a seat. I haven't seen you since the party. We've been running around like a couple of rats in a maze." She scooted back against the headboard and patted the bed. "Well, don't just stand there. *Asseyez vous*."

Feeling a little like a criminal meeting her executioner, Mollie sat down stiffly on the bed's far corner. "Funny you should mention rats," she said. "You must think I'm the king of them all."

Nicole looked surprised. "Why?"

"What do you mean, *why*? We both know why you broke up with Mark."

"So what's that got to do with you?"

"Everything!" Mollie cried. "If it weren't for me, you two'd still be dating."

"Oh, come on, Mollie," Nicole said. "I know you sometimes think the world revolves around you, but why should you want to take the blame for this? It's not your fault."

Mollie couldn't believe what she was hearing. "I don't understand...."

"Neither do I," Nicole said, observing with newfound curiosity Mollie's guilty expression and stiff posture. "Maybe you ought to tell me what you're talking about."

Mollie clasped her fingers so tightly her knuckles cracked. "I'd like to hear why you broke up with Mark first."

"Okay." Nicole ran her fingers through her hair and heaved a deep sigh. "At first, things were great between us; then a couple of weeks ago, I started getting a funny feeling whenever I was around Mark. It crept up on me, sort of like a cold you keep trying to hold off. But I think it all began when Mark insisted I audition for the play, even though I didn't want to."

"But I thought you tried out because of me!"

"That, too," Nicole said. "See, I didn't really want to try out, but I also didn't want to start a fight with Mark about it. Then when you told me you were nervous about auditioning alone, I decided to go with you, to keep you company."

"So you weren't disappointed when I got a part and you didn't?"

"Of course not. I told you that."

"I didn't believe you!" Mollie admitted. "I'm so wild about theater, I couldn't believe you weren't too."

"We're sisters, not identical twins," Nicole said gently. "Anyway, Mark was the one who was really disappointed. He even asked Ms. Black if she'd reconsider and find something for me to do. But he didn't bother asking *me* if that's what I wanted, and that was when I started to get the funny feeling." She shook her head. "It got worse when he put pressure on me to go to UCLA. College is practically a whole year away, but he acted as if I were abandoning him because I wanted to apply to other schools! That made me take a long, hard look at where our relationship was going."

"So your breakup had nothing to do with me. . . ." Mollie let the words trail into the air.

"No. But I'm really curious why you feel responsible."

"Uh, it's not important now," Mollie hedged, getting up and moving toward the door.

"Yes it is," Nicole said quickly. "It's why you came to see me, right?"

All Mollie could do was nod. For a brief moment she thought about making up some silly story. But in her heart she knew she'd never feel right unless she told Nicole the truth. She sank back onto the bed. "For the past week or so, I haven't been able to look at you cross-eyed without getting into trouble," she began. "Sometimes I knew what I'd done wrong—like ruining your shirt and lying about my French assignment—but sometimes I didn't. The worst was last Friday at lunch. You were so cold to me, I felt icicles coming out of your eyes."

"Friday?" Nicole was silent in thought. "Oh, I remember now. I'm sorry, Mollie. I wasn't mad at you. You just happened to be in the wrong place at the wrong time. See, Mark and I were in the middle of a fight over the amount of time we spend together. When you showed up, he used it as an excuse to change the subject. But I couldn't turn off my anger, and I guess you got caught in the crossfire." She sighed again. "It's not that I don't like Mark, but I liked things a lot better when we didn't stick together like Siamese twins. Too much of a good thing is just as bad as not enough, you know."

Mollie *didn't* know, but she thought it best to save that conversation for another day. As it was, she was glad she'd chosen to open up to her sister; Nicole's words were peeling away the layers of tension she'd felt for days. But she had one last unanswered question. "What about the kiss?" she asked quietly.

Nicole stared at her blankly. "What kiss?"

"The one Mark gave me."

"What?" Nicole felt a jolt in her chest. She'd never had reason to believe Mark was after her sister—but a kiss? "When did this happen?" she demanded.

"At the party." Mollie stared at her in surprise. "You know. You were looking right at us. I saw you."

Nicole shook her head. "I must have been lost in the ozone. I didn't see it. But why did he kiss you? What happened, Mollie?"

Mollie curled up on the bed as if she were trying to make herself smaller. "It all happened so fast I'm not really sure. I was coming from the family room when Mark bumped into me and asked me to dance. It was a slow one and he held me real close. Then he kissed me. After that I panicked and ran up to my room."

Even though she was through with Mark, Nicole still felt a pang of jealousy. The feeling didn't make sense to her, but then neither did the kiss. If Mark truly liked Mollie, he was a much better actor than she thought. She pondered for a moment. "Did Mark say anything to you about me?" she asked.

Mollie shook her head. "But there is one thing, now that I look back on it. Mark seemed sort of upset, and when he kissed me it was all of a sudden. He didn't lead up to it or anything."

Nicole's tense shoulders relaxed a little and she leaned back against her headboard. "Was this before or after Mark and I did that lip-synch duet?"

"After. After I did mine, too. That was really fun, wasn't it?" Mollie brightened for a moment, then her smile flattened. "Anyway, I remember that you were dancing with Duffy."

The pieces were starting to fit together for Nicole. "I get it," she said.

"Get what?" asked Mollie.

Nicole hesitated. She was afraid of hurting Mollie's feelings by telling her what she thought—that Mark had used Mollie to make her jealous. "Um, it's hard to explain," she hedged. "But it's all part of why I broke up with him."

Mollie was still confused. "What do you mean?"

Nicole sighed. "I hated the idea of breaking up, but midway through the party Mark did some things that showed me I had to cut the ties between us. I could see it wasn't going to work. He wanted a lot more out of our relationship than I did."

"Like what?"

"Well, I want to be able to plan—or at least think about—my future without him. But ever since his parents got divorced, he's been searching for something—some kind of guarantee, to hold on to. I don't want to be tied down like that, Mollie. I'm only seventeen! Anyway, you had nothing to do with us breaking up. Understand?"

"You still like him, don't you?" Mollie said.

"Sometimes liking a person's not enough," Nicole said sadly.

Mollie pointed to the pad. "Then what's that about?"

"I'm still trying to decide if I've done the right thing. Mark's taking it really hard, and it's painful to see him mope around and be miserable. Today at lunch he started to sit with me, and I had to tell him to leave. Do you know how much that hurt both of us?"

"Is there any chance the two of you will get back together?"

"I don't know, Mollie." She shrugged helplessly. "But I do know I owe you an apology. I've been so upset about Mark that I've taken some of my anger out on you. I can't let that happen again. Forgive me?"

Mollie couldn't believe it. Nicole asking *her* for forgiveness? "I'm sorry, too, Nicole. I should have come to you a lot sooner to clear things up." She leaned over to hug her sister, and Nicole hugged her back. But it seemed to Mollie that there was a little stiffness in the gesture, as if something were still coming between them. And in a flash of understanding she knew it was Mark.

Chapter 13

"*W*elcome back, Miss Lewis. It's nice of you to pay us a visit, especially as it's our first dress rehearsal. Are you going to stay?"

Mollie hung her head at Ms. Black's sarcastic greeting. It was well deserved, and she realized now how childish it had been for her to skip out on rehearsal. "Yes, Ms. Black," she said sheepishly. "Where do I go to put on my makeup?"

Ms. Black pointed to the rear of the stage. "We've set up two dressing rooms there. Come back out when you're finished."

Mollie nodded dutifully, then hurried across the stage, her costumes for the second and third acts slung over her shoulder. Now that things were nearly back to normal between her and Nicole, she felt like a new person. So even though she hadn't resolved her confused feelings about

Mark, she was ready to devote herself to the show with total commitment.

This was to be the first of two dress rehearsals, and Mollie was already wearing her costume for the first scene, having donned it right after dinner. Nicole and Cindy had looked on admiringly as she'd gotten into the car with her mother for the ride to school, and Mollie thought she'd never felt more proud.

Heather was already applying her makeup when Mollie entered the makeshift dressing room. "Glad to see you back!" she said with a big smile.

"This is one girl who's never walking out again!" Mollie vowed. "I can't wait to get started."

"Sounds like you worked things out with your sister."

"Yes—and you were right. It was a giant misunderstanding." Mollie eyed Heather's costume admiringly. "Where'd you find that?"

Heather had on a cream-colored sweater over a gray flannel skirt decorated with a large off-white fleece poodle. "My mom had it stashed away in our crawl space. She never throws out anything!" She nodded at Mollie's outfit. "You look very Sandy-ish."

"Courtesy of the costume committee—and the Salvation Army," Mollie said, swinging her plaid shirtwaist dress from side to side. "So where's the gang of four?"

Heather laughed. That was the name they'd given the other four girls in the cast, who never made a move without one another. "Who knows?"

she said. "In the meantime we've got the makeup table all to ourselves. Dig in." She made room for Mollie at the wooden table centered under a large lighted mirror.

Mollie began to apply her makeup with methodical precision. First, she blanketed her face with a heavy layer of pancake, knowing from her previous theater experience that she'd blend into the scenery without it. Then she turned to her eyes. Up close the heavy black eyeliner and bright blue shadow looked clownish, but under the bright glare of the stage lights, she'd look like a typical high-school girl of the late 1950s. After that she colored her lips a bright pink and then brushed her blond curls into a ponytail. And suddenly, magically, she'd transformed herself into Sandy.

Next to her, Heather was rapidly turning into Jan, the girl next door, coaxing her punkish locks into a headful of spit curls—with the help of half a bottle of styling lotion. Then the other girls entered the dressing room, too, and the cramped space was filled with chatter and a sense of expectation that something big was about to happen.

From the nearby boys' dressing room they could hear a medley of very moldy oldies. "Kenny brought that to help us get into the mood," Heather said, tying a bow in one of her white sneakers. "I hope it works on Mark and he snaps out of his slump."

"I'm sure he will," Mollie said, feeling awkward.

"He probably needs a little time to sort out his feelings, that's all."

"We don't have time. We go on for real Thursday night."

Mollie sighed. "It sure would solve a lot of problems if he and Nicole got back together."

"Spoken like a true romantic."

"No, I mean it," Mollie whispered so the other girls wouldn't hear. "You don't extinguish a fire like theirs overnight."

"I hope you're right. I'm a big romantic, too." Heather looked down at her body. "About as big as they come."

Mollie was about to tick Heather off for running herself down when she saw her friend grin. "Come on, short stuff," Heather said. "Let's go break a few legs."

Mollie linked her arm in Heather's and began to sing, "We're off to see the wizard, the wonderful wizard of Oz." Quickly she covered her mouth with her hand. "Whoops, wrong show," she giggled.

The rehearsal started without a hitch, and Mollie slipped easily into Sandy's character. This is the way it should have been all along, she thought as she jaunted around the stage during her first dance number. This is fun! This is magic! I feel like Dorothy setting off on the yellow brick road.

Of course it wasn't a perfect journey. She and the other cast members had to stop a few times because they bumped into unfamiliar set pieces or got into the wrong places for the dance numbers. But these sorts of delays were to be expected in any dress rehearsal. And Ms. Black, sitting in the front row, hardly glanced at her ever-present notebook. She was totally taken in by the show unfolding before her.

Mollie was performing the final song of the first act when it dawned on her that she'd paid hardly any attention to Kenny all evening. She turned to look at him and, to her surprise, felt none of the gut-wrenching aches she'd once thought were synonymous with his name. He was simply another boy now.

Right after that she spotted Jeff winking at her, but it was impossible for her to tell if he was acknowledging that he'd read her mind, or trying to flirt with her, or simply had a fleck of dust in his eye. There is so much I have to learn about boys, she decided. They are definitely too confusing.

After a short break for costume changes and makeup repair, they all reassembled for Act Two. Mollie was still feeling the rush that was a natural by-product of a show in progress, and for the first time she allowed herself the luxury of speculating what this production would mean to her social life at Vista. A little later, as she stood backstage during an early scene in Act Two, she saw a photographer and reporter from *Viewpoints* come in and sit down next to Ms. Black. Since she was the female lead, they might want to interview her—or at the very least feature her picture in the school paper! Mollie's arms erupted in goose bumps at the thought. Her first real press notices!

The idea, while appealing, was also alarming. What if she said the wrong things? What were the right things? Maybe she was better off not saying anything at all! Then she remembered reading an article in one of her magazines about a TV actress who became a star when her series hit the top of the ratings. She refused to grant interviews and, as a result, some of the scandal sheets started printing a lot of rumors about her. Wanting to stop them, she finally consented to talk, but what she had to say made her sound petty and vindictive.

Mollie wondered what might happen if she unwittingly said something that made her sound evil or ugly. It didn't take long to come up with an answer. No one would ever speak to her again. Her entire high school career would be over less than two months after it'd begun!

Indulging in such speculation made it hard for her to concentrate on her next scene. In fact, Ms. Black made her stop and do it over because she'd started speaking like a robot. Think like Sandy. Think like Sandy, she kept telling herself. Then came the Kissing Scene.

Mollie thought about Sandy and how upset she would be to discover that the boy she thought she loved wanted more from her than she could give. Why, that's what Nicole was talking about, Mollie realized with newfound understanding.

Mark, as Danny, was sitting next to her with his

hand draped over her shoulder. He started to move it southward, the way they'd rehearsed any number of times. But Mollie felt a new sense of dread wash over her like a sudden winter cloudburst. This wasn't Danny sitting next to her; it was Mark! The guy she'd been avoiding ever since their real-life embrace.

She could hardly bear to imagine what would happen next, afraid that when Mark kissed her she'd rekindle that strange, undeniably exciting feeling she'd experienced the night of the party. She hadn't been able to handle it then, and she didn't think she could handle it now, even though she was supposed to be acting.

And what would happen if she couldn't hide her feelings? She'd ruin Nicole's life, that's what. Mark's kiss would prove that he'd shifted his affection to Mollie, and not only would the entire cast see it, but everyone else at Vista would, too—thanks to the newspaper.

In her vivid imagination, Mollie saw it all flash before her eyes. *Viewpoint*'s photographer would capture the moment with his camera, and *National Enquirer*–style headlines would be splashed across Page One: GIRL CAUGHT IN REAL-LIFE LOVE TRYST WITH SISTER'S EX-BOYFRIEND. The accompanying article would be full of speculation about the real reasons why Nicole and Mark had broken up, and even if the reporter included a statement from Nicole, who would believe her when the proof was there, in black and white, that her kid sister felt something for Mark?

Mollie couldn't go through with it. Even though acting was one of the most important things in her life, it was only a *thing*, and it was meaningless compared to her feelings for Nicole. "No!" she shouted just as Mark was about to give her the kiss.

"You're too early," Ms. Black called out. "You're supposed to turn away after the kiss."

But Mollie had already started across the stage. And before anyone realized what was happening, she'd scooped up her purse and was racing out of the auditorium and out of the building into the overcast, starless night.

She didn't look back until she reached the corner and crossed the street to the bus stop. Then she turned and saw Mark and Heather making their way down the school's front steps. They hadn't spotted her yet, but they would, soon. Mollie felt herself break into a cold sweat. She couldn't let them catch her. She couldn't go back inside. Not now, not ever.

The lights of a metro bus came into view. Mollie dug into her purse and pulled out some change, praying the bus would reach her before Mark and Heather did. But just then she heard a shout.

"Look! There she is!"

Mark and Heather had reached the curb, but a steady stream of mid-evening traffic was preventing them from crossing to her side. "Mollie, what are you doing?" Mark called to her. "Come back. Are you crazy?"

Mollie didn't answer. The bus pulled up and blocked the two of them from her view. She hopped aboard and dumped all her change in the slot, not caring if she was paying more for the ride than she had to. All she knew was that she had to get away from there as fast as she could.

Chapter 14

"*H*ello, Nicole? It's Mark. I've got to talk to you."

For a moment, Nicole didn't know how to respond. She'd already told Mark, as nicely as possible, that she needed time away from him. Now here he was, calling her up. She didn't want to act nasty, but how else could she make him understand? "I'm busy right now," she said stiffly. It was the oldest excuse in the world, but at this point she didn't care.

"Look, I wouldn't be calling if it wasn't important. *Very* important," Mark shouted into the phone.

Nicole paused, suddenly aware of the frantic tone of his voice. "What's wrong?" she cried.

"It's Mollie. She ran away from rehearsal."

"What? Where did she go?"

"That's why I'm calling. I don't know. She hopped

on a bus a couple of minutes ago. My car was parked in the school lot and the bus was long gone by the time I pulled around. She's not at home, is she?"

"No," Nicole said, her own voice mirroring his concern. "What direction was the bus heading?"

"I don't know," Mark answered. "And I don't understand why she's doing this. But unless we find her within an hour, Ms. Black will throw her out of the show for good."

"I think I know where she might be," Nicole said. "Wait for me, I'll be right there."

Stopping only to put on her jacket and grab a set of keys, Nicole hopped into her mother's station wagon and raced toward the high school. She got within two blocks of the building before she was stopped by a red light. Two red lights later, she was still there, courtesy of a car that tied up traffic trying to make a left turn. Nicole pounded the wheel in frustration. If she'd been thinking clearly she never would have suggested picking up Mark. The school was in the opposite direction from the beach where she figured Mollie might be—and time was running out fast.

Finally, she pulled up in front of the school, and Mark and Heather piled into the car. Though her mind was filled with worry about her sister, Nicole was relieved she didn't have to make the trip with Mark as her lone passenger.

A few minutes later they pulled up at a bluff overlooking the beach, about two miles south of the main city pier.

"Mollie always comes here when she wants to be alone to think," Nicole told them.

But Mollie wasn't there.

"I think if she were coming she'd be here by now," Mark said. "She must have gone someplace else."

Heather looked at her watch in alarm. "How are we going to search Santa Barbara in thirty-five minutes?"

"Maybe we don't have to." Nicole snapped her fingers as a new thought entered her mind. "C'mon back in the car!" Quickly, they drove to the nearest gas station, where Nicole hopped out again and raced to a pay phone.

Cindy answered on the first ring. "Is Mollie there?" Nicole asked anxiously.

"Where are you?" Cindy countered. "Yeah, she came in about five minutes ago. She says she wants to talk to you."

It took less than five minutes to get back—Heather kept a running check on the time—and she was in such a hurry she forgot to close the car door as she dashed from the driveway to the front door. So Mark closed it for her, and he and Heather followed closely behind.

"Mollie, where are you?" Nicole called as she came inside.

"You don't have to shout. I'm right here," Mollie said meekly. She was sitting on the living-room sofa, surrounded by Cindy and her parents.

"See if you can talk to her," Mrs. Lewis pleaded.

"We haven't been able to get a word out of her since she came back."

Nicole looked at her sister. Mollie still had on her costume and stage makeup, and there were light blue streaks running down the sides of her cheeks, evidence that she'd been crying. "Why did you do it, Mollie?" she said gently.

Mollie began playing nervously with the sofa cushion. When she saw Mark and Heather enter the room behind Nicole. "Not with them around," she said.

Nicole walked over and took her hand. "Come with me," she said.

To everyone's surprise, Mollie agreed readily. She followed Nicole up the stairs to her sister's bedroom. "Sit down," Nicole ordered, pointing to the bed. "Now tell me what you think you're trying to do."

Mollie looked around the room, trying to avoid answering the question. She fixed her gaze on the map of France displayed prominently over Nicole's desk, wishing she could escape there right now. Any place would be better than this.

"We don't have much time," Nicole went on. "Ms. Black gave you an ultimatum. If you're not back in school in—" She looked at her alarm clock. "—twenty-three minutes, you're out of the show for good."

Mollie shuddered. It hurt terribly to be reminded of what she was giving up, but she felt she had to make the sacrifice. "I'm not going back," she declared, but it didn't sound as forceful as she'd wanted, coming out more like a whisper than a roar.

"Why not?" Nicole asked patiently. She leaned against her desk chair, arms folded, waiting for an answer.

"Because of you," Mollie whispered.

Nicole was completely taken aback by the unexpected reply. "What are you talking about?" she demanded.

"You wouldn't understand," Mollie said.

"Wait a second. You junk your big chance for stardom at Vista because of me, and I'm not supposed to understand. What are you trying to do, give me a guilt complex? Am I supposed to go through the rest of my life feeling I've ruined things for you—and not even know why?"

"Well . . ."

"Please, Mollie, something's obviously bothering you. Let it out. It can't be as bad as you think, whatever it is."

"I'm afraid," Mollie admitted.

"Stage fright?"

"Sort of," she hedged.

Nicole paced around the room, thinking out loud. "I guess it's understandable, given that this is your first high-school production . . . all those eyes on you, all the attention. But you've always thrived on that kind of pressure. Why are you letting it—"

"It's not the show itself," Mollie blurted out. "It's this one scene."

"Yes?" Nicole asked, trying to draw her out.

Mollie sighed. "It's a kissing scene between Mark and me. I'm afraid to let him kiss me."

Nicole stopped pacing. "I think you're confusing this with what happened at the party, Mollie. But it's different. It's just acting."

"It's *more* than acting," Mollie insisted, and then suddenly the words tumbled out. "I think I care about Mark and I know he cares about me, and I'm afraid that it'll come through loud and clear when we kiss on stage. If I go through with it, then everyone's going to think you two broke up over me. I can't do that to you."

"Whoa, there." Nicole joined Mollie on the bed. "That was quite a mouthful. Let's back up. What's this about you and Mark? You've never considered him more than a friend."

"That was before he kissed me. Now ..." She held up her hands as if to say everything had changed.

"Now what?"

"It's hard to explain," Mollie said. "It's true that till the party I never thought of Mark as anything but your boyfriend. But that kiss he gave me was—well, it was special."

"You've kissed boys before. What made Mark's kiss so different?"

Mollie shook her head. "I never kissed anyone else before."

Nicole's brown eyes popped open. "You're kidding!"

"C'mon, Nicole, I'm only fourteen. Who've I gone

out with? When have I had a chance to kiss someone?"

Nicole stopped to consider. "I guess you've always acted so much older, and whenever the topic of boys or dating or kissing came up, you always seemed so knowledgeable. I guess I just assumed. . . ."

Mollie hung her head. "So now you see what I'm up against. I can't risk kissing Mark again, even if it's only *supposed* to be make-believe. Besides, I don't want to do anything that will mess up your chances of getting back together."

Tears welled up in Mollie's eyes, and Nicole suddenly felt very old and wise, as if a lot more than three years separated her from her sister. "You've got a bunch of different problems all tangled up together," she said, "but maybe we can sort them out. First of all, forget about Mark and me. Whether we get back together or not is *our* business—not yours. Our decision will have nothing to do with you, or with that kiss." She eyed her sister sternly. "Do you understand that?"

Mollie nodded meekly.

"Okay," Nicole went on. "Then second of all, do some thinking about that kiss. I remember that my first kiss was a pretty big deal, but you've made a soap opera out of yours! Try to put things into perspective, Mollie, and consider this, too: if you're really serious about being an actress, you'd better learn the difference between a stage kiss and a real one, or you'll be falling in love every time you take on a new role!"

She looked at the clock. "Think about it, Mollie, but think fast. It'll take us at least five minutes to get you back to school." And with that she left the room.

Mollie sat there for a few moments, debating what to do next. She thought about going back to her room, her little haven against the real world. But it wasn't in her nature to be a recluse; the stage was where she really belonged. Then again, she'd made a big fool of herself that evening. She couldn't imagine Ms. Black wanting her back now. And she still hadn't resolved things with Mark. She brushed away her tears, smearing her makeup even more. How had her life turned into such a disaster?

She took a few steps toward the door, still not sure which way she was going to turn, when Mark came running up the stairs.

"Mollie," he called. "I've got to talk to you. Right now."

Again, Mollie was torn. One part of her wanted to shut the door in his face. But another part— the part she had a sneaky feeling was the growing-up side of her—insisted that she talk with him. She leaned against the door frame. "I've really messed things up tonight, haven't I?" she said softly.

Mark shook his head. "I'm the guilty one," he said, nervously running a hand through his hair. "I'm sorry, Mollie."

"What for?" Mollie asked.

"For giving you the idea there could be something between us. I like you, but not like that."

"What about the night you took me out after set building?"

"I—I was just being friendly. You were having such a hard time with those nails and all, I sort of felt sorry for you."

Mollie flushed. She didn't like being pitied, yet at the same time she felt relieved. "And the kiss?" she asked.

Mark shifted from foot to foot, unable to meet her eye. "It was a dumb thing to do. Uh, not that I don't like you, Mollie. I do, and I've had a great time acting with you." He combed his fingers through his hair again. "This is hard for me to say, but the truth is, I kissed you because I wanted to make Nicole jealous. I was mad at her and hurt that she wanted to dance with Duffy instead of me, and you happened to be there. But I never figured you'd give it a second thought. If only I'd known ..."

A host of conflicting emotions washed over Mollie: anger that Mark had used her, and dismay that she'd misunderstood his intentions so completely, but above all, relief that despite the feelings his kiss had given her, there really wasn't anything but friendship between them. "Actually I was *afraid* you liked me," she said. "I—I'd never been kissed before."

A slow smile spread over Mark's face. "I was your first?"

Mollie nodded. "And I blew it way out of

proportion—I see that now. But at the same time, since it felt nice, I thought that meant I had to be in love with you."

"You mean you're not?" Mark said, pretending to be shocked. "I'm crushed—but Mollie, does this mean you're ready to go back to rehearsal?"

"There's one thing I want to do first," Mollie said seriously. "I know this is going to sound strange ... but would you kiss me? I've got to see if it feels the same the second time."

Mark complied, giving her a quick brush on the lips. Then he pulled back and looked at her inquiringly.

"Nice," Mollie said reflectively, "but nowhere near as special as the one on Saturday night."

Mark laughed. "I guess there's nothing quite like a first kiss," he said.

Mollie sighed. It would take a long time for her to lose the feeling that she'd acted like a total fool. But the only way she could keep from being an even bigger fool was to get back to rehearsal as soon as possible. "Do you think Ms. Black will buy a bad case of stage fright?" she asked.

"It happens once to everyone," Mark reassured her. "There's no reason why she'll ever have to know the truth."

"Then what are we waiting for?" Mollie said ecstatically. "It's show time!"

Chapter 15

*T*wo nights later Mollie stood center stage under a spotlight, surrounded by applause from a tightly packed auditorium. She'd never heard anything quite like it before, and to her ears the clapping was as loud as a sonic boom.

She still felt the stage fright that had been with her since the opening scenes, the jitters that had made it seem as if an electric mixer were stuck in the "on" position in her stomach. But along with it was an enormous sense of relief. She'd made it through the show—and people had liked it. At least that's what she *thought* the applause was about. The bright stage lights kept people's faces hidden from view.

Just then Mark grabbed her hand and led her to the stage apron, where they bowed to a new round of applause. She looked at her co-star and matched him grin for grin. After all, they both had a lot to smile about. Opening night had been a big success, and they had two more performances to go.

Mollie wished she could have held on to that moment forever, but all too soon the curtain came down again. Mark was still holding her hand, and she felt a slight resistance as she tried to pull away to join the rest of the cast.

"Hang on a sec, Mollie," he said. "Before you go, I just want to tell you that you were terrific out there tonight."

Mollie felt a blush of happiness rise underneath her layer of pancake makeup. "So were you, Mark. And I owe you special thanks. If you hadn't gone after me the other night, I wouldn't be here."

Mark grinned. "What are friends for? Speaking of which, I've got something for you." Gently he planted a soft kiss on her forehead.

For once Mollie took it in the spirit in which it was intended. In turn she gave him a kiss on the cheek. "Thanks for giving me my first stage kiss," she told him.

"It wasn't that scary after all, was it?"

"No," she admitted. After all was said and done, by the time she'd reached that critical scene, she was so absorbed in the role that she'd actually reacted to it as Sandy, not Mollie—the way it was always meant to be. "I bet it'll be even easier next time," she added.

"Same time, same place tomorrow night, okay?" He winked.

"Is this a private party?" Heather's booming voice filled the air.

Quickly, Mollie turned around and fell into Heather's open embrace. "We did it, kid," Heather cried.

"I couldn't have done it without you." Mollie felt the first sign of tears welling up in her eyes. *I can't cry,* she thought. *I'm happy.*

"I'll remember that when you're famous," Heather declared. "Come on, let's go get out of this greasepaint."

Mollie's walk to the back of the stage was interrupted by congratulations from the rest of the cast. After receiving hugs and kisses from the gang of four, she looked up and saw Kenny smiling at her. He gave her a thumbs-up sign and then slipped away to the boys' dressing room.

She saw Jeff standing near the curtain and walked over to him. "What's with the sad face, Marshmallow? You were great tonight."

Jeff sighed, pulling off the varsity sweater that had been part of his costume. "I always hate the end of a show. All the planning, all the work, and then—poof—it's over."

"Aren't you jumping the gun? We've got two more shows to do."

"They'll be gone like that." He snapped his fingers. "Then it'll be back to the same old routine again."

Mollie knew what he meant. After the cast party Saturday night, everyone in the production would be going their separate ways. And suddenly she realized how much she'd grown to care about these new friends of hers—even the funny boy standing right in front of her.

"Uh, Jeff, I never got a chance to tell you how bad I felt about walking out on you at my sister's party," she said. "It didn't have as much to do with you as ... well, it's a long, complicated story, and I'd rather not go into it. But I, um, I guess what I'm saying is I hope we can still be friends."

A slow, tentative smile grew on Jeff's face. "I've got this great joke about a grizzly bear. See, one day in the woods—"

Smiling, Mollie held out a hand. "I want to hear all about it—but at the cast party, okay? I see some people waiting for me." She stepped around him and ran to her parents, who were standing with Cindy and Grant at the entrance to the girls' dressing room.

"Mollie!" Mrs. Lewis cried, wrapping her youngest daughter in her arms. "You were so wonderful!"

"Thanks, Mom," Mollie said. "I hope I did the Lewises proud."

Her father hugged her and handed her a bouquet of pink roses. "I hear it's traditional to give flowers to the leading lady," he told her.

"They're from us, too," Cindy said, mussing up Mollie's hair. "I guess I can't go around calling you my dumb kid sister anymore. You were really something!"

"Thanks," Mollie said.

"But there was one thing I was disappointed

with," Cindy went on. "There wasn't nearly as much kissing as I thought there would be."

"Remind me to tell you a story sometime," Mollie said to her sister. Then she became aware that someone was missing. "Where's Nicole?"

"Over here." Nicole was standing several feet away from the others.

Mollie handed her bouquet to Cindy. She had a feeling Nicole wanted a few words with her in private. "Excuse me. I'll be right back," she told her family.

As Mollie walked closer, Nicole brought her hands forward to reveal a beautifully wrapped box tied with a red ribbon. "I thought you'd like this," she said. "Read the card first."

Mollie pulled the envelope out from under the ribbon and removed the card. On the front was a picture of a unicorn standing beneath a rainbow. Inside, Nicole had written in her neat, flowing hand, *To my sometimes crazy, often dramatic, and always caring sister. Never stop daring to dream . . . but don't let your imagination get the better of you. Love, Nicole.*

Inside the box was a delicate white porcelain drama mask, with red satin ribbons tied to the sides. "It's beautiful. Thank you, Nicole." Mollie hugged her sister tightly, and this time she felt nothing but love between them. Tears welled up again, and she sniffled, powerless to stop them. "I must be catching a cold or something," she said.

"Or something," Nicole repeated knowingly.

Mollie smiled through her tears. "You're the best sister a girl could have," she said.

"Better not let Cindy hear you say that," Nicole teased. Then she turned her sister around and gave her a gentle push toward the dressing room. "Now hurry up and get rid of that war paint. It's time to party."

"All right!" Mollie called happily over her shoulder. "I have a lot to celebrate tonight."

Here's a sneak preview from SECRETS AT SEVENTEEN, the next book in Fawcett's "Sisters" series for GIRLS ONLY.

Early Saturday morning when Cindy came down for breakfast, she found Nicole already up drinking coffee and pacing the kitchen.

"Something the matter, Nicole?"

"What?"

Cindy shrugged as she took out the milk and orange juice." I know when you're upset. Sure you don't want to talk about it?"

Nicole paused for a moment and sipped some of her coffee. Her lips parted as if she planned to say something but changed her mind.

"You going somewhere this morning?"

"No." Nicole's voice cut the air like a knife.

"Sorry I asked." Cindy backed off, and then decided to try again. "Well, you don't usually wear makeup on Saturday mornings. And you don't usually get up so early. Some new guy you want to impress?"

Nicole pressed her lips together and shook her head. Cindy could tell that she had just washed her hair, because the scent of the lilac soap Nicole always used pervaded the air.

"I told you, I'm not doing anything special."

"Then what are you waiting for?"

"Nothing."

"Why are you pacing?"

Nicole shrugged and poured nearly half the carton of milk into her coffee.

Seeing that her sister wasn't going to answer, Cindy sipped her own milk and then carefully asked, "Nicole what . . . I mean, do you ever see Mark?"

"Mark?" Nicole looked surprised. "No. Why?"

"Well, I was wondering . . . I mean, you and he were pretty close. What happened? You never really told me."

Nicole shrugged. "I didn't think you were interested. Nothing happened." She smiled at her sister's puzzled look. "I mean, I liked him and all, but didn't . . . we didn't . . ." She waved her hand, gesturing, and her face took on a dreamy expression. "He was nice, but when you fall in love there are"—she sighed—"special sparks that come between you and him." Nicole smiled at her sister again. "You'll understand when you're older, Cindy. Why's everybody asking about Mark all of a sudden?" She finished her coffee.

"What are your plans for the day?"

"Going to the beach." Cindy poured some milk into her cereal bowl. "Looks like a real hot day—the surf, I mean." she said, noticing her sister's quizzical expression. She paused and watched her sister. "Bitsy's joining Anna, Carey and me. Now that you haven't been spending any time with her, I guess she feels left out."

"Bitsy?" Nicole's blue eyes went big. "Why? I mean, she has other friends besides me. And she's not even in your crowd. You never really liked her before."

Cindy shrugged. "She wants me to teach her how to surf, and I guess she also wants to know what's going on with you. You have been acting rather strange lately. You've canceled tons of things with her. The two of you used to do everything together." Cindy paused. "What should I tell her?"

"Tell her . . ." Nicole paused. "Tell her that I've more important things to do." Her eyes shone as she touched her younger sister's arm lightly. "Oh, Cindy, I have great plans. And I want them to be a surprise."

"What plans?"

Nicole sighed. "I can't tell you yet. But I will. I promise. Soon."

The SUNSET HIGH SERIES...for Girls Only!

by Linda A. Cooney

What more could a girl want?

At Sunset High, the most prestigious high school in Beverly Hills, students are the offspring of movie and television stars, producers, musicians and writers. Life is sophisticated and glamorous—but there are down-to-earth problems, too...